Advance Pr&
We're Not ᴋɪcn

"*We're Not Rich* captures the subtle intricacies and explosive moments of disappointment, grief, love, and love lost that make us human, all laced with brilliant humour and gorgeous revelation…all the big, too-human catastrophes coupled with the searing moments of sweet clarity that get us through. Murtagh is fleet and sure, every word exacting and right; her characters flit through rage and broken attachments and tenderness and insight—an astoundingly talented writer, a gripping and utterly beautiful collection of stories."
LISA MOORE, author of *This is How We Love*

"*We're Not Rich* is a thrilling debut, shimmering with tension and truth. These are the stories we long for—note-perfect accounts of the ways we falter and fail and somehow, miraculously, endure."
ALISSA YORK, author of *Far Cry*

"Where does it go? Our money, our love, our youth, our trauma? And what are we supposed to do now? Like the rest of us, the characters in *We're Not Rich* are carried, and moved, by these timeless questions. This is seriously great writing, but don't worry: Murtagh is hilarious too. Furious and forgiving at the same time, this is one of the best collections we've seen in a long, long time."
ALEXANDER MACLEOD, author of *Animal Person*

"The stories of Sue Murtagh are reminiscent of those by Raymond Carver or Denis Johnson—seemingly quotidian on the surface, but beneath those seemingly placid waters they roil, and seethe, and speak to us the hard truths that many of us would rather not confront."
CRAIG DAVIDSON, author of *Cascade* and
The Saturday Night Ghost Club

"Sue Murtagh's debut short story collection is sensitive and brilliant. From her precise, carefully wrought descriptions to her note-perfect inner monologue, Murtagh navigates complex and at times devastating subjects, from a mother losing her son to a fraught teenage friendship to a secret family history of Holocaust resistance. Her stories often contain a great deal of dark wit and wry humour, from marriages that fall apart to intricate sibling dynamics to navigating adult dating. In fact, the whole collection is so sophisticated and assured, it's hard to believe that it's Murtagh's first. A wonderful read."
DANILA BOTHA, author of
Things That Cause Inappropriate Happiness

"These stories, with their threads that travel from narrative to narrative, characters who occur and reoccur, relationships that change and evolve, satisfy with a novelistic scope, while the writing is tight and focused on the moments. Sue Murtagh writes tough storylines with confidence and ease, heart and heartbreak in equal measure.
I loved this collection."
STEPHANIE DOMET, author of *Fallsy Downsies*

We're Not Rich

Vagrant Press is an imprint of
Nimbus Publishing Limited
3660 Strawberry Hill St, Halifax, NS, B3K 5A9
(902) 455-4286 nimbus.ca

Nimbus Publishing is based in Kjipuktuk, Mi'kma'ki, the traditional
territory of the Mi'kmaq People.

Printed and bound in Canada

*These stories are works of fiction. Names, characters, incidents, and places, including
organizations and institutions, either are the product of the author's imagination or are
used fictitiously.*

Editor: Alexander MacLeod
Editor for the press: Whitney Moran
NB1725

Library and Archives Canada Cataloguing in Publication
Title: We're not rich : stories / Sue Murtagh.
Other titles: We are not rich
Names: Murtagh, Sue, author.
Identifiers: Canadiana (print) 2024040176X | Canadiana (ebook) 20240401778 |
ISBN 9781774713402 (softcover) | ISBN 9781774713419 (EPUB)
Subjects: LCGFT: Short stories.
Classification: LCC PS8626.U78 W47 2024 | DDC C813/.6—dc23

Nimbus Publishing acknowledges the financial support for its publishing
activities from the Government of Canada, the Canada Council for the Arts,
and from the Province of Nova Scotia. We are pleased to work in partnership
with the Province of Nova Scotia to develop and promote our creative indus-
tries for the benefit of all Nova Scotians.

We're Not Rich

stories

Sue Murtagh

For Sandy and Katie, and our beloved Ben.

Stories

Rescuing Spiderman

IT'S THE FIRST DAY OF SPRING, BUT REMNANTS OF SHRIVELLED, blackened snow litter the community pool parking lot. You're here to try a swim. The so-called experts claimed this would help you. To be precise, they said it could help you, should help you, but at first it might hurt. They promise it will not harm.

So here you are—you try to please—wearing the royal blue Speedo with the tummy ruching that you bought because it seemed correct to begin with a new bathing suit. You've chosen to launch this (supposedly) healing habit at the midmorning lane swim. You remember from your past life that at this time of day, the pool is quiet. Just a handful of lumpy people muddling through the strokes in chemically treated water that could irritate sensitive skin.

Today, there's an exception. In the first lane, a woman with powerful shoulders in a black, racerback bathing suit is plowing through the water at a furious pace, only turning her head to breathe every fourth stroke. At each end of the pool, she somersaults underwater and pushes off the wall. It dizzies you just to watch.

There are just four others, each meandering down their own individual lanes, separated from their neighbours by red plastic lane ropes. The only vacant space is in the middle. You would have preferred to stick to the outside, but this is all there is, so you kick off your flip-flops and sit on the edge of the pool. The water feels cool on your legs. You focus on the circling red hand of the large, analog pace clock sitting on the deck—it measures time in seconds only—before you lower your torso into the water. What was cool on the legs feels harsh on your arms and chest. You can smell the chlorine.

You have a difficult time finding your rhythm. Your front crawl seems off, your breathing laboured, so you attempt breaststroke, hands together as if in prayer and arms in a V as you glide. That doesn't work either. Your goggles are too tight but at least they don't leak. They allow you to see the pool bottom and the concrete walls at the ends of your lane.

A Band-Aid on the pool floor drifts into sight. Spiderman's red masked face stares up at you, fixating with his blank white eyes. He is large enough to cover a gravel-battered knee after a six-year-old runs into trouble. Some kids are unusually accident prone. You had one of those and you went through many boxes of superhero Band-Aids.

You assumed Josh would turn out fine because you put in the work. You weren't a "jellyfish parent" or a "brick wall parent." You and your husband learned to "talk so kids would listen and listen so kids would talk."

Smug you and your smug friends, all of you slurping up everything those parenting manuals dished out. Suckers.

You make it to the end of the lane, turn around and push off the wall to swim back. You don't know how long you can keep this up. Before everything, you used to easily handle fifty lengths, four times a week.

On the way back, the Band-Aid is in the same spot, but Spiderman has flipped. Now he's a bloody rectangle floating like a cartoon ghost. You swim over.

You can't remember if they advised you to concentrate on being in your body or to be a mechanical doll. You pick doll, mechanical swimming doll, because you don't see any other way to continue, and you must continue.

But the Band-Aid lingers. Instead of drifting out of sight, it remains always beneath you on the pool floor, and as your strokes create ripples, the Band-Aid turns. Plastic side up, then bloody side up. The crimson mask alternates with this brownish stain. This breaks your doll-like rhythm.

You imagine the bandage loosening, then falling off a little boy's knee during family swim. No one noticed, or maybe they pretended not to notice so they wouldn't have to deal with it. With every length of front crawl, every time you swim over it, your chest tightens. You could switch to back-stroke so you don't have to look but you choose not to.

The pressure in your diaphragm builds. *You came here to relax—all you wanted to do was relax—they promised this would be good for you. Relax. Relax. Relax.*

But this Band-Aid. It must go.

You stop to alert a lifeguard. There are two guards on duty; one appears to be in his late teens, the other in his early twenties. Look at them—they move through the world in adult bodies with adult freedoms, but they're still burdened with the frontal lobes and impulse control of teenagers. They have zero concept of the permanent consequences of their actions.

The older one is tall, dark-haired, and bearded. The brooding kind. He looks familiar but you can't place him. The younger one is scrawny, skin raw with acne. In another time and place, your heart would break for him.

You pick the skinny one. You tell him about the Band-Aid. How gross it is, where it is. At first it seems he will help. He asks you to point out the exact location, so you do head-up breaststroke, you stop and wave, gesturing that the spot aligns with an orange caution cone on the side of the pool. You want to make it easy for them to collect this debris. He nods and you continue your swim, expecting he'll need you to get out of the way when he or the other guy cleans up. The skinny lifeguard approaches the bearded one. They confer, they part. You do a bit of breaststroke. You want to be reasonable, give them the benefit of the doubt, but you can't wait.

"The Band-Aid," you say to the skinny one when you finish that lap.

He tells you the long pole with the little net on the end—the skimmer—won't reach that far.

"We'd have to drain the whole thing," he says.

That's just the stupidest thing you've ever heard. Ridiculous. He is lying to you, lying.

You say exactly this. What kind of people are they hiring these days? You say this too, which prompts him to wave over the other guard.

"If he can tear himself away from his phone," you say.

When your Josh patrolled this pool deck it was different. He'd be in that water in a minute. Jump in. Jump right in without thinking.

The bearded guard arrives to impart his wisdom.

"The net won't reach," he says.

"I'll do it," you offer, to shame them, and they're too lazy to even shrug.

You do your best head-up crawl back to Spiderman. Before you dive, you look back to the pool's edge where the young men still stand. Bearded One wears a dumb smile, while Ravaged Face bears no expression other than stupidity. You, a taxpayer, are paying these useless specimens to watch you dive for someone else's garbage. They'll probably laugh about you at break time. It turns your stomach. You know you look like some entitled hag, but you don't care.

The Band-Aid hasn't moved but reaching it is difficult. On the first try, Spiderman eludes your clumsy hand. You pop to the surface to see the guards still gawking. Claustrophobia circles, panic will smother you. But you try again. You channel the mechanical doll. Long, slow inhale, long, slow exhale before you dive. You move deliberately, you don't grab. You see the hairy kicking legs of an old man two lanes over.

This time you succeed. You spread your fingers like a net to block off escape routes and close your fist around the plastic. Spiderman caught in the palm of your hand.

Your task is complete; this moment should feel good, but the used bandage seems inconsequential. You swim toward the edge. It is not easy to swim with one clenched fist. You dump the Band-Aid on the pool deck. The younger lifeguard reaches over to collect it. You notice he now wears a blue medical glove to protect his precious hand. The other guard just walks away.

That's it. No one thanks you, of course. No one cares.

And then you realize who the bearded lifeguard is. He was three feet shorter when you first met him. You're sure you know this kid. He is one of the four Adams who were in Josh's class. There were always multiple Adams—in hockey, in basketball, in the school band. For years, all you did was hand out granola bars and juice boxes to Adams. Even then, this one stood out as whiny and sullen. He was invited to birthday parties when the thing to do was to include the whole class, but he was never one of the boys Josh invited over after school or on weekends. Not a friend.

A current of adrenalin races from your feet to your heart, your pulse pounds. There's sudden, excruciating heat on your damp skin, and yet again you can't catch your breath. You raise your body out of the pool. Now you are on the deck. You approach the wall. Hanging horizontally is that scoop they claimed wouldn't work, that they refused to even try. It looks like a giant butterfly net.

You tear the scoop from the wall and throw it like a spear, watching it fly awkwardly into the water. It lands well into the deep end of the pool, which is roped off because people aren't allowed to swim there at this time of day.

The aluminum pole bounces gently, silently, and then floats. This is not satisfying.

You spy the plastic bins of pool noodles they use for aquafit class. These hollow tubes, in green, pink, and orange, are insubstantial weapons, inadequate, but they're all you have. You launch your missiles one by one. Airy foam, they land lightly on the surface of the water and barely make a ripple.

You try a life jacket, grabbing one from a metal box that looks like an open-topped cage. You lift the jacket over your head and throw hard. This jolts the muscles and tendons in your shoulders, strains your ragged, worn-out rotator cuffs. Fluorescent yellow flies twenty feet and lands daintily, with minimal impact, the straps splayed on the water surface. What you need is a deep hard splash, a thud, a rogue wave, a tsunami. Instead, all this brightly coloured buoyancy cheerfully decorates the deep end.

The lifeguards finally notice and come after you. Women your age are invisible until they make trouble.

You point at the mess.

"Is there enough crap in there now to get your arses into the water?"

"That's disrespectful," the guard who must be Adam says. "Not appropriate."

"Whoop dee fucking do."

In the old days you never used this language. You were the endlessly patient mom with the constant smile, handing out melting ice cream cake and disappointing Dollarama goody bags. *Where did that get you?*

You notice the scoop pole is no longer completely afloat. It tilts at forty-five degrees and may yet sink to the bottom.

"You little fucker, I know who you are."

You see him seeing you, shaking his head, and you know. You know he does not recognize you.

———

THE LIFEGUARDS RADIO me to help them deal with another breakdown on the pool deck. These clowns can't handle anything by themselves. For this, I get an extra $2.58 an hour, a cubbyhole office behind the front desk, and a hand-me-down nametag with no name on it, only *Daytime Rec Supervisor*.

Yesterday it was a middle-aged perv with greasy hair who hung around on the pool deck, playing with his phone. He needed the Wi-Fi, he said, but the guards claimed he plunked his butt on a bench and stared at the junior swim team. Mega creepy.

I told the guy that the library had better signal strength and it was just down the hall.

"On you go," I said.

Today I hear the problem before I see it. A woman's voice, angry.

"Why the fuck are you here?" she asks. "You're useless."

Good question. I sometimes ask it myself.

"Why?" this woman repeats, almost shrieking. Her voice strained to the breaking point.

I know her as soon as I hit the deck. It's Josh's mom. I only met her once and I was one of hundreds streaming past the family that day, but it's her.

Screaming, poking at Cory: "Why you?"

Then sticking her finger in Adam's face: "And why you?"

Coat hanger shoulders, under a layer of pale, wet skin, and her blue swimsuit is too big. Spiky, salt and pepper hair sticks up from underneath the straps of the black goggles wrapped around the bones of her skull.

I call her by her name: "Mrs. LeBlanc."

She freezes, then wobbles like someone about to faint. I don't feel too steady myself, but I offer my hand.

"I'm Sarah," I say. "I worked with Josh."

I doubt this sinks in, but an instinct for politeness draws her hand to mine like muscle memory. Her palm is damp and cold. I hold on tight and lead her away from those gaping idiots.

We walk across the pool deck. In the back corner, there is a sauna, a square wooden box that looks like the top of a tree-house. There's a sign on the door with "Out of Order" hand-written in black marker.

"It will be better in here," I say, leading her in. "This is private."

She has transitioned from yelling to a kind of dazed confusion, and comes along passively, as if this is not super weird.

I close the sauna door and we sit on the lower bench.

"And maybe let's take off those goggles," I say.

She does what I ask. The goggles leave deep purple indentations around her eyes, as if someone punched her twice. Maybe she doesn't know that it's the suction that keeps goggles from leaking, not death-grip tightness. Or maybe she just doesn't care anymore.

I take her hand again and rest two fingers on her wrist to check her pulse. Her heart is racing. I ask if she has tightness in her chest, pain in her arms. Yes, she says. She has pain in her chest every day, all day.

"Do I know you?" she asks. "Or, how do you know me?"

I repeat that I worked with Josh, that we took our certification course together, that we were weekend morning shift partners. Buddies. We used to take breaks right here, in the sauna, which was broken most of the time because the maintenance guy was and still is a tool. Her bruised eyes show a flicker of life and interest as I talk about her son. If someone tells you a new story when there can be no more new stories, it's a gift.

"We'd hide out. He always made me laugh," I say, and that's mostly true, the exception being at the end, the last few months, when he'd come to work still half-wasted from the night before. She doesn't need to know that.

Then she unreels this tale about a filthy Band-Aid stuck to the bottom of the pool. I nod at the right times. This is not the moment to break the news that there's always crap down there and sorry that's just the way it is.

Her words come slowly, as if she struggles to construct a story from long ago, details fuzzy. And then she stops mid-sentence and slumps, chest collapsing onto her thighs. I realize that my fingers are still on her wrist and that her pulse has slowed.

I'm tempted to tell her about my brother, but don't. There's a fine line between empathy and saying "I know just how you feel" when you can't possibly know.

It always pisses me right off when someone jumps into their own shitty tale. Shut up for a few minutes and let me have my own story. This isn't the Pain Olympics.

I say, "Mollescum contagiosm."

Mrs. LeBlanc's free hand flies to her cheek.

"Oh, you know," is all she says, but she sits up properly again, and I think her jaw muscles soften.

"Sure I do."

Mollescum contagiosm. During our first shift together, Josh told me that he came to a birthday party here when he was seven or eight. A week later, he broke out in the grossest bumps. Red, round, and shiny, they covered his arms and chest. He had to smear on smelly cream for almost a year, and every few weeks the doctor burned off new growths as they erupted. Kids at school made fun of him.

The next time I heard that story, at a work party with a proper audience, he played it for laughs. "Bumps from the top of my head to the crack of my ass," he said and we all roared.

"He never complained, oh but I was so angry," his mother says.

In her version, some kid came to the pool with the virus and it was her son—only her boy—who caught it. Josh was in the same pool doing the same things that everyone else was doing, but he was the only one who got nabbed. It was a one in a million thing.

"It wasn't fair," she says. Sitting so close, I can see the faint wrinkles above and below her lips. There are deep lines around her dark eyes that meld with the goggle bruises.

I tell her she isn't wrong. "None of this is fair."

In a fair world, we would sit together in peace. But this is the real world and the wooden box we're hiding out in isn't soundproof. A muted but still crappy Coldplay song drifts in as the warm-up for aquafit begins.

She starts to talk again, tells me that a few days ago she rummaged in Josh's room. Her husband warned there was nothing new in there since the last time, but she was restless.

"I had no idea what I was looking for," she says.

In Josh's top dresser drawer, shoved under the flannel pyjama pants she gave him that final Christmas, tag still on, there was a stack of swim instructor material.

"Certificates, and all the coloured badges. Blank lesson plans. My husband was right. Nothing new."

Now I can't help myself and I tell Josh's mother about my younger brother. I don't insult her with the "I understand" line; I just say what happened. I'm not looking at her face anymore. I'm looking down at my fingers on her wrist, relieved that her heart rate hasn't sped up again.

"If he'd known what it really was, he wouldn't have taken it."

She doesn't speak, just sighs, a prolonged intake of breath followed by an eternal exhale.

I finish by saying, "Nowadays, I write in a journal. Sometimes I go to a group."

I don't tell her that on the darkest days, when I'm furious and want to hurt someone, I choose to hurt myself. I call in sick and close the drapes and drink Mike's Hard Lemonade and binge Netflix all day in dirty sweatpants. I don't tell her I still have nightmares about the morning the cops came to my own mom's door. Or that now I keep Naloxone in my car and at my apartment, that I double-check our pool supply at every shift.

Instead, I blurt: "Bring it all in."

"What?"

"Those swim badges and the rest of that stuff. If you bring it to the pool, we will take care of it. You don't need to worry about it anymore."

She nods and asks if she can go to the change room now; she wants to go home. I tell her she is allowed back in the pool whenever she's ready, that I'll talk to the guards. Maybe next time will be better.

"I see myself do these things," she says. "I yelled at some girl on the bike trail the other day because her stupid German Shepherd wasn't leashed. 'Oh he's well-trained, he's friendly,' she blabbed, and that just set me off."

The goggle marks around her eyes are fading. I get up and she follows.

"Don't forget to bring me the box."

"Yes. Someone should get some use out of all of it. Otherwise, such a waste."

The truth is, if she does part with all of Josh's leftover lifeguard crap, it is just going to end up in the garbage. I don't tell her this, but the Lifesaving Society changed everything, chucked out the old learn-to-swim program months ago and brought in a new one. There are no colours anymore. Only numbers now. I might store the carton in the swim office for a few days, but the dumpster out back is where it is headed.

At least Mrs. LeBlanc won't have to look at it anymore.

I lead her to the change room.

"On we go," she says, and her tone has the forced cheer of a weary Girl Guide leader heading out on a hike. She pushes through the door on her own.

On my lunch break I go outside. The pool, my office, all of it is suffocating.

The pervy pool guy from yesterday sits on the next bench, hunched over his phone, hood pulled up over a grimy ball cap. What I told him is true: the Wi-Fi really is stronger out here. It floats invisibly over the wooden benches, even slightly into the parking lot, where people with no internet at home or limited data know they can connect for free. Every day, they appear before the library doors are open and stick around in the evenings, long after closing, even in cold weather when the garden is nothing but rocks and dead leaves.

My logical brain knows this guy has a right to be here. He's just trying to pick up a signal. But today he makes me angry. I look over at him, concentrating so hard on whatever it is he holds in his hand, and all I can see is someone taking up a space. That spot, the exact place where he is right now, I think it should be reserved for others.

Lost Purse

THERESA MISPLACES HER PHONE EVERY SINGLE DAY. DITTO HER car keys. But after the regular panic and flurry, running around like an idiot upstairs and down, dialling the phone from the land line, checking yesterday's pockets, she always finds what she's looking for. The wasted time sticks around, though. Makes her late for work. Or for visiting hours at the hospital. Or errands for her mother.

On Tuesday, she had a miracle half-hour to herself, so she walked around the Halifax Commons after her ICU visit. When she got back to the car, there was a ticket on her windshield and, oh yes, keys locked in the trunk. She was forced to walk to the hospital and ask her oldest sister, Peggy, to use her CAA membership to send help. Then she waited by the car in subfreezing temperatures for forty-five minutes until the tow truck guy arrived with his wedge and the fancy coat hanger. Took him less than a minute to open everything back up.

Last month Theresa lost her Visa card, and then the replacement was hacked by someone who spent $193 on shoes before hitting her $3,000 credit limit. Stray five-dollar bills appear in her jacket pocket, but cash she swears was in her wallet evaporates. Also missing: two earrings, a hairbrush that could use a cleaning, and her work lunch bag. Her 2012 Fiesta has a two-foot scratch (deep, almost a dent) on the right side, and a gouge on the bumper from hitting the same concrete parking post two days in a row. She missed three chiropractic appointments, and her left shoulder is coiled into her neck, which presses like a jagged rock against her skull. Turned up for a haircut at the right time, wrong day.

Sitting in the Fiesta in front of her mother's apartment building, Theresa realizes two things. First, she cannot recall the drive. Travelled eighty kilometres an hour down the Dunbrack connector, and unaware of it. She has no memory of something that happened thirty seconds ago.

Second, no purse. No purse.

It is a purple Roots crossbody bag that her three sisters chipped in for. A quality item, they point out. They aren't the shy types. One of them told her, "It was expensive, even on sale."

"At that price, they should throw in a wallet of cash," their mother said. "Theresa, you take good care of it."

She had the bag not five minutes ago, but situations turn in an instant. You have something, then it boom vanishes. Gone.

She remembers flying into the Spryfield Sobeys to buy canned tomato soup, evaporated milk, Metamucil, and Red Rose teabags. At the cash register, Theresa held up the line because she couldn't find her Scene card. Then had to dig around for the car keys. Maybe she put the purse on her shoulder. Maybe into the cart with the loose groceries—her cloth bags are in a dirty pile in the trunk of the scarred Fiesta.

Then what? She has no idea.

Theresa drives back to Sobeys but she can't remember where she parked the first time, so she cruises the lot. People pull into parking spaces and pull out; they jockey carts over the icy pavement, prepare to buy what they need. Families. Stuffing their trunks with chicken and eggs and frozen chunks of potato.

Other lives continue, she thinks.

After her third circuit of the lot, Theresa begins to understand this is futile. She gets out of the car and stops a teen boy in a Sobeys jacket who's collecting stray shopping carts.

"Have you seen a purple purse? I lost my purse," she says. His tiny eyes move down and to the side.

"Nope. Check inside with Customer Service."

As she approaches the store's automatic doors, a harsh northwest wind whips her face. It seems to her the shopping cart kid must be lying and she predicts that Customer Service won't care either. They've seen it all. The misplaced receipts, the spoiled milk, the rejected credit cards. We all have troubles.

THERESA HAS A key to her mother's apartment but buzzes anyway, and is surprised by Peggy's voice crackling on the intercom. When she gets upstairs, she finds her sister on the couch, folding their mother's socks and underwear, still warm from the dryer. Making herself at home and making herself useful. Peggy explains their mother wanted to be on the move, already drove to the hospital by herself and insisted that she wait for her sister.

"Jesus, I'm only fifteen minutes late," Theresa says as she drops the groceries on the kitchen counter.

"You know how she is."

Theresa doesn't want to tell Peggy about the missing bag, but she has no choice. No surprise that her sister quizzes her about what's in the purse. Wallet, credit card. Maybe health insurance, a few points cards. Peggy immediately wants to write a list.

"You need to organize yourself, Theresa. Think."

But Theresa can't be precise about the purse contents

without a side trip home to check which cards are in her dresser drawer.

"Right, okay, let's go do that," says Peggy.

"No time. We're already late."

"He's not awake, Tree," says Peggy. "There's no rush."

Theresa hunts through her mother's cupboards until she finds baked goods. She curls up on the couch in her heavy coat and pries the lid off her mother's cookie tin.

"I think he can hear us," she says, examining a burnt gingersnap, her father's favourite, and offering the tin to her sister. Peggy takes a handful of cookies and shoves Theresa's legs aside to fit into leftover sofa space, putting her sock feet up on Mom's coffee table.

"Tree, at least cancel your credit card," Peggy says after a few minutes.

"No, not now. Later."

After her fifth cookie, Theresa thinks: Pictures...our Christmas pictures are on that phone. She should have backed them up. She meant to back them up but didn't. Told her kids no don't do it for me, I will do it myself. She really meant to. Theresa tries hard to remember exactly what will be lost. Hundreds of images embedded in four inches of plastic and metal and she can't even conjure up one.

"We should call Mom," Theresa says. Neither sister moves until the northern cardinal on the Audubon wall clock chirps three o'clock. Theresa uses the land line to phone the hospital. She tells their mom they're running late and about the lost purse.

"How much money was in it?" her mother asks.

"None," says Theresa.

"No money? None? Tree, you need money," says her mother.

"No cash, Mom. It's all the other things, replacing all the other things," Theresa says before passing the phone to Peggy.

WHEN THEY GET to the hospital, Theresa and Peggy see their middle sisters—the away sisters —for the first time. One just flew in from Calgary and the other drove from Moncton, with a stop at the airport. The away sisters brought tea and muffins.

An ICU nurse invites them to a private waiting room. Their family name is typed in capital letters on a piece of paper eased into a metal slot on the door. It is a small kindness. Families granted a private room will only need it for a few days. Then a nurse will remove the old piece of paper and slide in a new one with another family's name.

Theresa's mother updates the newcomers after they settle in.

"Theresa lost her purse."

Everyone is retired except Theresa. The Moncton sister asks her how she's managing with work. Will these missing days make it harder to get hired on full time at the call centre?

"I'm on vacation," Theresa lies. She is a part-time employee, still on probation, so she has no vacation days.

In the hospital waiting room, drinking lukewarm tea, they tell stories, sharing favourite scenes like movie reviewers. Peggy brings up the time Theresa hit her head on a patch of schoolyard ice and went missing for two hours.

"You were right out of it," says one of the middle sisters, and the others laugh but Mom doesn't.

THERESA THINKS OF the snow boots they all wore. The stench they gave off. Clodhoppers with the hand-me-down sweat of her siblings and a half-dozen Maritime winters. By the time she got them, no grip at all.

Remembers fishing the boots from a jumble of rubber and fake fur by the radiator. They were meant to fit over her despised black oxfords. The frustration of squeezing leather shoes into damp galoshes that buckle at the ankle.

Late, always running late. Then clomping into the battleship grey of a Halifax February.

Pixie face and pixie hair framed by a Kmart pom-pom hat, she joins a band of the similarly heavy-footed and they all thump past Peggy in the alley, who is shivering in a poncho and passing a cigarette to a pale hippie Jesus called Donny. Past the corner store that takes her allowance on Saturday mornings. Over and through snowbanks, to a red-brick prison named after a saint.

Midmorning—a brief liberation—heavy wooden doors push open into salt air. She leaves her sweater, mitts, and hat in the cloakroom.

Theresa sails across the ice, sheets of dull diamond. The fastest runner in the schoolyard, boys included. Then a tumble up and back. Horizontal now, on a patch of hardened soil. Still and silent. A rush of colour comes into focus: blue-white sky, a wildfire of hair, green eyes more curious than concerned. She closes her eyes against the light, but itchy wool fingers brush her cheeks to interrupt. The faces are closer. A brittle ache sets in as the buzzer orders their return. The crowd scatters back to the classroom.

All except Theresa, who just wants to go home.

She loses herself on the winter sidewalks of the neighbourhood. She must be close to home but the clouds in her head block the way, so she keeps walking. Wanting to be home because she knows he is home, back from crawling into boilers and turbines in Cape Breton and New Brunswick. She's used to the schedule, takes both his absences and his presence for granted. He doesn't wear a suit and work in an office. He doesn't work in a factory either, but he knows how to fix things.

Maybe half an hour later, a plainclothes nun looks across a sea of navy tunics and yellowing blouses and notices an empty desk. She finally calls Theresa's mother.

"Imagine that. And you missing since recess," Mom says, now wedged between the two away sisters on the waiting room couch. She looks across to Theresa and shakes her head. "That woman was useless. Useless as the day is long."

The February snow that Theresa wandered in that day was not the stuff of fairy tales. The snowbanks that lined the streets were hard and sooty. She paused to lean on a blackened pile. Leotards drooping and jacket hanging open, bare hands pressed against needles of ice. Nausea—up came breakfast. Fragments of raisins and Cheerios, toast with strawberry jam on the dirty snow, on her cold fingers.

"You puked your guts out," says Peggy, breaking the last chocolate chip muffin in half.

This is where the Chevy Impala found her, six blocks from the school. He wore his brown tweed fedora, no mitts on his massive hands as he scooped up Theresa with a speed that dizzied her dizzy head and she felt for a split second the roughness of his unshaven cheek as he held her tight and then it seemed she was thrown across the bench seat in the back of the car.

Time slowed again. The motor ran but the car stood still. She saw her father's blue eyes in the rear-view, looking back at her.

"Little Tree. Sweet Jesus," he said.

Theresa twisted to look back. Snow fell. A weightless camouflage to cover her humiliation. Gentle and careful, it blanketed the debris. In the car, the dry heat blasted and the wipers began their rhythm. The warmth and the swishing back and forth. She faded away. He always kept that car so hot.

Back in the hospital waiting room, her feet sweat in her fleece-lined Sorels.

"Yup," she tells her sisters and her mother. "I was right out of it."

Peggy's phone rings. The purse has reappeared. The call is from a woman named Beverly who found it, and thanks to decent phone hacking skills, called her big sister's number.

"It's a miracle," says their mother. "It's a blessing. See?"

Instead of passing the phone, Peggy takes down the details. She doesn't ask the questions Theresa would have asked. Annoying. Their mother tells them to get going for god's sake. Nothing will happen while they're gone.

Peggy drives. The woman lives close to where they grew up, off the Herring Cove Road. It is a subdivision carved out of a gravel quarry where Theresa and her sisters used to smoke and drink before school dances. The city made a land swap with a developer and now all the houses cost a million dollars and there's a new walking trail. The homes, each different but all the same.

"Christ, imagine the property taxes," says Peggy as they pull into the driveway.

When Beverly opens the door, Theresa recognizes her. This Beverly, who now goes by Beverly Holmes, used to be Bev Murphy. They hung out a bit in high school. Bev Murphy made out with just about anybody who muckled onto her at a dance. Beverly Holmes wears Lululemon and has a dream kitchen that smells like homemade beef stew and hot biscuits. She doesn't recognize Theresa until Theresa says Tree MacDonald.

"Oh Tree, my god," she says and invites them to sit at her kitchen island.

They leave their boots on a rubber mat at the front door but keep their coats on. Beverly tells how she found the purse in a dirty pile of snow next to the Sobeys parking lot. How she was leaving the grocery store when she spotted it by the exit near the gas station next door. It was the colour that caught her eye. Something didn't look right so she stopped her SUV to check it out.

"Seemed like it was nothing," she says. "But I picked it up and checked inside it and thought, 'this woman must be worried sick. Just worried sick.'"

The good news is, nothing is missing, but Theresa wonders what Bev/Beverly who lives in this house with the cobbled walkway and the symmetrical shrubs thinks of Tree/Theresa's purse. The fabric lining has grimy edges and pen marks. Contents include wrinkled grocery receipts, balled-up tissues, earbuds with tangled wires. Her call centre swipe card.

"The cap was missing from your hand cream so I put it in a baggie," says Beverly. "But there was no money when I found it. Looks like whoever stole your purse just wanted the cash and chucked the rest."

"Well it's only money," says Theresa.

"Well la-dee-da," says her sister. Beverly laughs.

They should leave. Theresa ignores her sister's dirty look and takes in the kitchen's neutral toned paint, ivory cupboards, granite countertops, and stainless steel appliances.

"The things we got up to in high school," Theresa says.

"That time your father chased Billy up the street with a baseball bat. Running after that poor bastard in pyjama pants and rubber boots," says Beverly.

Bev, with an epic blonde perm and three coats of Midnight Black mascara, was there that night in grade ten when a half-dozen of them were kicked out of a dance after Billy McKenna spewed lemon gin on the vice principal. Somehow, they ended up at Tree's place. They could sneak through the back door and into the basement. There was an old couch and a few chairs down there, and a Ping-Pong table.

Her father sat at the kitchen table eating a slice of cold Kraft pizza, drinking Ten Penny from the bottle. Doing the crossword in an undershirt and baggy pyjama pants. Waiting up on a sticky June night, the screen on the back door letting in a slight breeze.

Billy was the first one in. Tree behind him, head spinning from Blueberry Mist chugged on the way home, arms around his waist, her hands tucked into the front pockets of his hockey jacket. Attached.

He pushed open the screen door, turned his head and then body to kiss her. Open-mouthed, lots of tongue. Tree tasted the gin vomit in his spit. Bev and the others pushed and crowded from behind, shouting and laughing.

"Holy shit," said Billy as he saw her father get up from the kitchen table to come after them. Sliding bare feet into dirty boots. Grabbing the baseball bat they kept at the back door.

BEVERLY ASKS HOW their parents are doing. Are they keeping well? Peggy explains what's going on, and then Beverly insists on giving them homemade tea biscuits and a container of the stew bubbling on the stove. When they try to refuse, she won't hear of it and fills a Tupperware with stew and a freezer bag with biscuits.

"Your mother always sent me home with something," she says.

At the door, Theresa notices there's a "For Sale" sign on the front lawn, whipped back and forth by the sharp wind. How did she miss that on the way in?

"Are you guys moving, Bev?"

"I guess so but no idea where or when. My husband hooked up with some girl."

She points at the sign.

"Now I have all this shit to deal with. I don't know."

Peggy does that thing Theresa can't stand, the sympathy head tilt.

Beverly hands over the food.

"Mortgaged up the wazoo. He can't afford to keep it. Me neither."

She walks them to their car, not bothering with a coat despite the frigid wind. Beverly waves as they pull away. After five minutes the car is hot—almost unbearable. Peggy likes to crank the fan. It is dark and seems very late, but it's only six. They really should check in with their mother and sisters, but they'll be there soon. And they can't change anything that might happen in the meantime.

Theresa holds her purse close. They will never learn how it ended up in the gas station snowbank. She'll shine up the scratches with a special leather cream she bought.

Rush hour, but they're driving against the traffic on Herring Cove Road. Cars approach in a steady stream. People fighting to get home through a bitterly cold winter night that has only just begun. The car reaches the roundabout that leads back to the peninsula of Halifax. The flow of this endless stream changes depending on the time of day. They wait and watch for an opening.

"Biscuit?" says Peggy.

"They're still warm," says Theresa. She opens the bag, breaks one in half, and lays a piece in her sister's outstretched hand.

"Rubber boots and a baseball bat." Peggy breathes the words as she chews the soft dough, lifting her shoulders and rolling them backward in her parka.

Theresa turns down the fan so she can hear herself think. She looks at the waves of headlights.

"And he's yelling so loud the whole street can hear. Billy's shitting himself. 'You keep running, you son of a bitch. Just you keep running.'"

She hands Peggy the second half of her biscuit.

The oncoming glare is blurry and distorted. There's a brief lull in the relentless circle of vehicles. This is when you're supposed to make a move, but the timing and location are important. Peggy guns it and their car slides safely into a lane between two SUVs. They make it around to the other side. A few more kilometres, a few more intersections, and they'll be back at the hospital, with him, again.

Insufficient Billable Hours

BEVERLY HOLMES CLAMPS HER MOUTH SHUT DURING MacDonald, Moran, and Cochrane's mandatory harassment awareness training. Better to let the younger ones talk. Most of the people in the room, unlike Bev, are lawyers. Look at them competing for the "most enlightened professional" award, she thinks. Lots of clever chatter about diverse viewpoints, cultures, and lifestyles. Excellent, fabulous. But what about the guy who never, ever, bothers to put a lid on his vegetarian chili in the lunchroom microwave? Leaving someone else, namely Bev, to clean up. Or the articling student who ignores the "full" light on the paper shredder. Someone else, guess who, must drag that garbage bag to the recycling room, leaving a trail of confetti.

These are the offences Bev would prefer to discuss, but the lawyer in charge of the training, a specialist in labour and employment matters, happens to be the vegetarian chili guy.

After the final person has showcased their virtues in a self-serving statement disguised as a question, Bev stays behind to collect the empty coffee mugs. She crawls under a side table to reach a wadded-up napkin laden with someone's saliva. There she is, rump raised, clutching a damp, germy sample of colleague DNA, her bare, clumsily shaved knees scraping the blue-toned commercial carpet, when one of the senior partners surprises her.

"Hey, Bev."

Her startled head jerks involuntarily, slamming the top of her skull into the underside of the table.

Bev recognizes the voice and the narrow, pointy toes of the black suede boots.

"Ouch," says Izzy Mac.

Bev crawls out from under the table and hoists her body upright, irritating the tattered meniscus in her left knee. Head down, she leverages her good knee and two hands to stand. It hurts as she steadies herself. She wonders if her supposedly healthy knee is now going bad; it absorbs the pressure and signals with a sharp pain.

"Workers' comp," she says to Izzy, rubbing the tender spot. "See you in a few months."

Izzy Mac is piling grapes and melon on the last clean plate. She never eats during meetings, remains pristine while others end up with cinnamon sugar on their fingers, crumbs on their work wear, remnants of chewed food clinging to their teeth. But she always returns later to forage and take food back to her office.

"No strawberries left," she says. "Let's order more next time, yes?"

Bev knows there will never be enough strawberries. They'll keep coming back for more until they are all gone.

When Elizabeth (Izzy) MacDonald and Kent Moran, the two original partners, started the firm thirty years ago, it was just two lawyers, with Donna Albert as the paralegal and Bev as receptionist. They locked the door and went to lunch every Friday together at a pub on the corner. Nearly three decades on, there are nine partners, sixty-three associates, and a few dozen other employees who support them.

Or, as the partners refer to Bev and the others, "non-lawyers."

No one goes out to lunch anymore, at least not as a group, but a few months ago Izzy took Bev to Starbucks for Administrative Assistants' Day. When they had finished their caramel lattes, she handed Bev a flowery gift bag. Bev briefly hoped for a gift certificate somewhere useful, like Sobeys or Superstore or Canadian Tire. Nope. It was a book, *Get in the Driver's Seat*. The cover blurb mixed sad words with happy words.

Stuck, stale, trapped. Empower, take charge, rejoice.

"For the negativity," Izzy said. "Helped me."

"Did it? Really?"

"Kind of."

Bev regrets confiding: the separation, having to sell the family home with her freshly updated dream kitchen, how her boys hated squeezing into a tiny apartment when they came home from university on spring break. She should have weaseled a doctor's note after Bob left, instead of dragging herself into the office. But even that would have been a temporary reprieve, given their measly sick benefits. Fuelled by necessity, she subjects herself to the ritual of shower, coffee, protein shake on the commute from her Clayton Park apartment. Battle for a parking spot in a downtown garage, stare straight ahead in a crowded elevator for eighteen floors, boil a kettle, turn on the computer, and deal with her inbox.

Today, Izzy's heaping plate of leftovers was supposed to be Bev's lunch. What to eat instead? She usually keeps an emergency Lean Cuisine in the lunchroom freezer. Was it alfredo noodles with chicken? Or maybe she'll go out. Suzanne from accounting might want to get souvlaki from the diner in the basement of the office building. That would be good, and maybe some of those stuffed grape leaves on the side.

"Here's a list of the employees that HR came up with for our anniversary," Izzy is saying. Bev chucks the soiled napkin into the garbage can. Her fingers are sticky with residue from the napkin and the dozens of dirty plates she has stacked, and they cling to the white papers, leaving grease stains on the clean document that Izzy passes her with spit-free hands.

She's a civil litigator but Izzy is also responsible for special projects at the law firm, which means Bev has been tasked with a mishmash of work they can't bill clients for. Izzy's latest crusade is employee appreciation. She's planning a rah-rah session for the firm's thirtieth anniversary, which means Bev will have to organize it.

"We need to pull together something awesome," says Izzy.

Bev glances down at the clump of paper and sees *Donna Albert, paralegal, Employee #1*. Bev is listed as *general admin, Employee #2*.

———

DONNA ALBERT AND the former Bev Murphy, now Holmes and soon to be Murphy again, met on the Dartmouth side of the Halifax–Dartmouth ferry on the morning Bev quit her first adult job.

Just about every day, her boss at the community development office crept up as she typed on the IBM Selectric. He would put his nicotine-stained hands on her twenty-one-year-old shoulders, ask if she was tired, and then massage her neck, his untrimmed fingernails digging into her skin. He was old, in his midforties she guessed, and married to a pale woman with a frizzy perm encased in a cheap gold picture frame on his desk.

The third person in the office, Darla, that was her name, didn't seem to notice the sneaking up and the touching. She sat next to Bev at a melamine table in front of a second typewriter, head down and picking out one letter at a time. It was only the three of them in a makeshift office with used furniture and threadbare carpets, each hired on a government grant. Bev was hired under a new graduates' grant. She thought maybe her coworker was brought in on a program to get older women back in the workforce. Or maybe off the streets. She was what Bev's mother would describe as a hard ticket, and wasn't chatty.

"Indoor work and no fuckin' name tag," Darla had said on Bev's first day, by way of job orientation.

They were supposed to create projects to encourage small businesses to open downtown. The shoe repair place, pawn shop, and convenience store on the block had been there for decades. The office was on the second floor of a building that was eighty years old. It lacked both the modern convenience of air conditioning and the old-fashioned but practical charm of windows that open.

Bev's parents gave her an electric fan for her desk. Darla said, "Excuse me, Lady Di" when she brought it in, but the fan didn't help. They never do. Bev began each day wearing a blazer or jacket with padded shoulders, but made sure the blouse she wore underneath covered her arms.

"My boss is a perv," she told her mother.

"Cover up then," was her mother's advice.

One August day, the boss called her into his office. He was holding a letter Bev had typed. A letter to acknowledge the new owner of the shoe repair shop, which was passing from father to son. The boss was waving the letter like a flag.

"Do it again," he said. "There's a spelling mistake."

The boss had blotted out the word Congratulations with a black marker, the ink bleeding through the thin paper to the other side. Scrawled underneath was "Congradulations."

"But that's wrong," she said to the boss, who less than an hour ago had touched her again, startling her as she sat in front of the typewriter. Inquiring if she was a natural blonde. Fingering her neck until she stood up to go the bathroom.

Bev said, "I'm sorry, but that is not how you spell that word."

The boss said, "Yes it is."

Bev said, "Congratulations. I can look it up and show you."

"If I say that's how it's spelled that's how it's spelled."

"Because you're the boss."

"Bingo."

What happened next was not a conscious decision, was not premeditated. It was an uncalculated reflex.

"Well then, I guess you're not my boss anymore."

"What? Just who do you think you are?"

"I'm the person saying 'fuck this fucking job and fuck you.' That's who I am."

"You filthy-mouthed little bitch," he said.

Something had unlocked and it was easy, now, to stare at him. To examine the spittle leaking from the corner of his mouth. Behind his dry, chapped lips, she glimpsed a dull grey filling among crowded, discoloured teeth.

"Forget about a reference," he said. "Don't you ever show your face around here. Don't even try."

The thin fabric of his ivory, short-sleeved dress shirt was faint yellow under the arms, coordinating with his stained incisors. The shirt fabric was coarse and flimsy, almost see-through. She was tempted to say, "Hey, I can see your nipples."

He was still yelling as she left his office, "Who'd even want your useless ass?"

Bev walked to the communal work table and nodded to Darla, who somehow managed to keep her head down and look up at the same time. Picked up her purse, lunch bag, and her second pair of shoes. She left the fan for Darla, turning the breeze in her direction. Crossed over the musty carpet to the hallway, down the stairs, and into the sunlit street, stumbling a little and then regaining balance. She walked briskly in her high heeled black pumps; a power surge propelled her down the street to the Dartmouth ferry terminal. It was the fastest way to reach the other side of the harbour, and home.

At the terminal she dug a dime out of her purse. Tried to stuff it into the payphone. Dropped it, picked it up, and dropped it again, and finally dialled her boyfriend Bob's work number. But then hung up and took back her dime. Bev fumbled in her purse for a bit more change and went to the concession stand in the waiting area just as the ferry was starting to load.

She bought a root beer Popsicle and took it to the top deck of the ferry, where she sat alone on a long bench in the cool wind and sunshine. The ferry was a water bus that skimmed across the harbour; you could be in a different city in just ten minutes. She kicked off her heels, let them fall to the white floor. She wiggled her pantyhose-covered feet, working her big toe through to make a tiny hole.

Donna Albert, all dressed up in a navy blue skirt suit and bow blouse for a job interview with two young lawyers, saw it all and joined her on that long bench.

To look back on it, Bev feels it wasn't the most terrible thing, the worst thing, what her boss said and did. Certainly not an unusual thing in those days. And if she cried in the ferry terminal, clutching the extra shoes and the lunch bag and the purse, she doesn't remember.

What sticks in her mind is the feel of her toes on the ferry deck, the icy relief of the Popsicle, and Donna.

—

FOR THE LAW firm's thirtieth anniversary, Izzy says the partners brainstormed and came up with an idea that they all love. They want to highlight the music, movies, and major news events from their first decade.

"A tribute to the nineties," says Izzy. "They're looking for a PowerPoint with wow factor. Video and special effects."

Bev works hard not to roll her eyes. A PowerPoint? A frickin' PowerPoint?

They're sitting on the couch in Izzy's office.

"I'm really looking forward to working on this," Bev lies.

The employee list that Izzy gave her the other day is attached to her clipboard. To Bev's eyes, it glows radioactive. She meant to say something about the list at the beginning of their meeting, to ask if the partners had checked it, or even read it.

"Sarcasm, Beverly, is the lowest form of wit," says Izzy, doing that thing with her pen, waving it like a finger. "Focusing on helping others can take your mind off your own problems."

Bev scrolls through Wikipedia on her phone.

"Oklahoma City. Monica Lewinsky. O.J. Simpson. Real party material," she says.

She remembers Donna standing in front of the boardroom television, pulling people in whenever there was a CNN-worthy event, shaking her head at whatever tragedy or drama they were witnessing together. Donna, watching police cars chase a white Ford Bronco on a Los Angeles freeway, hand over her mouth, asking, "What is this?"

Bev continues her Google search, bent over her phone.

"Or if you prefer decade number two," she says, "we have 9/11."

Everyone in the office, side by side, watched the second plane hit, and then Izzy and the other partners sent them all home to their families. That was the last time Bev can recall them shutting down the office during business hours.

"Come up with a workaround, Beverly," Izzy says, as if Bev brought this up just to be difficult. As if the only things worth remembering were the fun times, memories you hand-picked to recreate a rosy past that never actually existed.

LUNCH HOUR AND Bev is at her desk. The chicken with noodles tastes like the box it came in. It triggers Bev's acid reflux; she can already feel the burning at the back of her throat as her esophagus rebels against this imitation of food. Bev eats it with a plastic fork and searches YouTube for video clips from nineties movies.

Clueless. 10 Things I Hate About You.

She sees Izzy walk down the hall toward one of the other partner's offices. Maybe on her way to complain about Bev. Seems paranoid but when they want you out, they find a way, and they execute the entire operation immaculately.

Dazed and Confused. Good Will Hunting. Misery.

She has been involved with the process many times, has typed and printed the paperwork. This is how they do it: You will arrive at the office to find an electronic calendar invitation for 9:00 A.M. It will have a generic subject line, something like *Meeting* or *Discussion*. You will be directed to the boardroom, where you will find two of the firm's partners. A blank-faced HR person will be the note-taker. Someone will read you a letter and then hand you a copy. They will want you to sign the letter, to accept a package for being let go "without cause." They will provide outplacement counselling and you'll get a year of benefits. There will be a payout based on your length of service. In some places, they attempt to chintz on the payout, but these are smart lawyers and they have done the math and figure that a few extra months of salary are worth it because the person they are dumping inevitably consults a labour expert at a rival firm. You need a number high enough so that the other lawyer confirms it's not worth fighting and will advise to take the deal.

My Cousin Vinny. Pulp Fiction. She's All That.

Termination without cause. There weren't many but she remembers each one, all the names and faces of the people who abruptly disappeared from the office, their desktops wiped clean overnight. How it seemed easy to slap a dollar value on two or five or twenty years of a person's life. A calculation based on age, length of service, and salary determined their worth. It all came down to simple math, interspersed with neutral, generic phrases, arranged in tidy paragraphs, proofread on a computer screen. Documents that Bev laser-printed on heavyweight, archival-quality cotton bond, tucked into a folder marked Confidential, and presented to a partner for signature.

Bev twirls a gummy noodle around her fork. Maybe it wouldn't be so bad, she thinks, to have someone dropkick you into the unknown.

AS USUAL, THE parking garage smells like pee. Bev climbs the stained, chipped stairs of the seven-level facility where she pays $250 a month to park her 2009 Corolla. She really should buy a bus pass but clings to this luxury she can no longer afford. Her joints ache on her trek to the top level. The concrete is unforgiving and her worn-out Clarks offer no relief.

Although the parking garage is open on three sides, daylight eludes it. By late afternoon the light is so dim that even shiny new cars lose their gleam. At the end of each row, there's a notice, "Small Cars Only," and in smaller letters, "Violators will be Ticketed." Every day at least one massive vehicle hogs these end spaces, making it tricky for everyone else to manoeuvre the tight corners. Today it's a black SUV, its front grille sticking out like an aggressive, bared grin.

Bev should walk on by. Let it go. But she flips, turns back to the staircase. There's a flutter in her chest; she is light-headed and knows she is light-headed. At the top of the stairs, a box with a small window at chest height is jammed next to an automatic pay station. In the box sits the parking attendant. Bev bangs on the glass. The attendant reminds her of her sons' gamer friends, zombie-pale from days spent in darkened rooms duelling strangers on other continents, controller in hand. But this likely basement warrior holds a paperback. He slides open the Plexiglas window.

Bev tells him there's a huge SUV parked where it shouldn't be.

"It isn't right," she says.

"Make and model of vehicle?" asks the attendant. His ParkRight coat is too big, a team jacket Bev assumes was assigned by an indifferent supervisor. The seams sag on his shoulders.

"A black SUV, the kind with the rings."

"Audi," says the attendant. His computer could be new but looks ancient. Everything in the glass cube is smeared with a layer of dinge. He opens the drawer again and rummages until he finds a pad of tickets and slaps up the "back in ten minutes" sign.

By the time the attendant opens his cubicle door, Bev is a few steps ahead, moving quickly, reaching the parking space just before he does. The Audi has vanished, leaving only grease stains and a balled-up Doritos bag.

The two of them stand in the empty spot. The ParkRight guy takes a pack of gum from his pocket. He offers her an old-school stick of Juicy Fruit, its shiny tinfoil wrapper peeking out from canary-yellow paper.

She thinks her head will surely explode; brain shards and shrapnel will bounce off the garage's impenetrable ceiling and scatter on its rigid floor. She accepts the gum and holds it in the palm of her hand, examines the glinting foil.

"Shit. Am I a tattletale now? A parking lot tattletale?"

The attendant unwraps his gum and rolls the greyish stick into a tidy spiral before putting it in his mouth. He stows the Juicy Fruit wrapper and his ticket pad in a pocket of his baggy coat, which appears to have grown another size over his narrow shoulders and chest.

"What does that make me?" he asks.

THE NEXT DAY Bev hides out in her cubicle. She tries to concentrate but doesn't make great progress on the anniversary PowerPoint presentation. Somehow, she erases a chunk of her morning's work and must recreate it all in the afternoon.

At 4:08, she gets an email from Izzy Mac. Elizabeth L. MacDonald, according to the firm's official stationery.

Please step in before you leave.

Bev packs an emergency bag. If they fire her today, however they label it—with or without cause, reorganized, downsized, modernized, or just plain laid off—she doesn't want to be supervised or scrutinized while she packs up her desk, and she refuses to have some junior HR flunky pack it up tomorrow in a cardboard box and FedEx it to her apartment. There isn't much to put in the reusable bag she keeps in her drawer: a travel mug, lip balm, a portrait of her boys before they grew body hair, a photocopied Halloween photo of her and Donna dressed as pirates. The program from Donna's memorial service, where Bev counted attendees from the office and eighteen months later can recite who was there and who was absent, screw their pathetic excuses, screw their sick leave stinginess. A half-empty box of Kleenex, a baggie of expensive imported tea bags she'd removed from the office kitchen because people took and took and never replaced. The rest—a few "certificates of appreciation," broken pens, stale cough drops, a squeezable stress ball with the law firm logo, a mountain of paper files she should have shredded years ago—it can all wait for someone else to throw away.

After a brief hesitation, Bev puts the memorial service program back in the desk drawer. She already has one, at home. Leaving this copy here means someone, whoever cleans out this drawer, will have to look at it, and decide.

Bev gathers her emergency bag, coat, and purse so she can exit the building or be exited from the building, directly from her boss's office. She takes a few steps, turns back, and shoves the thirtieth-anniversary file into her bag. She knocks on Izzy's partly closed door, and peeks in. Izzy waves with one well-manicured, neutrally polished hand and keeps typing with the other. Bev puts her belongings on Izzy's couch and sits opposite her boss, who offers a candy dish with tiny red and blue balls. Milk and dark chocolate. When Bev nods no, Izzy picks one out for herself but doesn't unwrap it, just rolls it around on the desk top.

"Things aren't going well, are they?"

"I've tried—"

"I make a case for you almost every month to keep this role. But it's getting tight. Now the other partners are asking what the hell are they getting for their money," says Izzy Mac.

"I don't—"

"At this point, to them, anyway, not me of course, you are overhead. Nothing but. No billable hours."

When Izzy Mac's first husband, a legal aid lawyer, left her for a bearded environmental activist named Frank fifteen years ago, Bev sat by her side on the chocolate-brown leather couch in this office, put a light hand on her shoulder, and watched her sob. Kept vigil for hours. She drove Izzy home that day in Izzy's car, and Bob had to come pick her up.

Today's Izzy looks at Bev with clear green eyes on a face whose freckles are methodically erased, every winter, by the pulsed light of an aesthetician's laser.

"When they ask you, when we ask you, to take ownership of an important task, isn't it a reasonable expectation that—"

Bev holds up an index finger.

"Right," she says, rolls her chair over to the couch, digs out the file from her bag, and rolls back. The sheet of paper Izzy gave her the other day is clipped to the folder.

"This list. I'll run it down to your suck-up buddies in HR, ask if they can spot the employee who no longer walks the earth," says Bev, pushing the paper across the wide desk. She has highlighted Donna's name in neon pink.

"Did you even notice? Seriously."

Blood rushes to the surface of Izzy's fair skin.

"Bev, I'm so…I don't know, so…"

Bev raises herself from the swivel chair.

"Donna and I went to yoga at lunchtime. She taught me how to knit. She taught you to knit too, didn't she? I was there."

Izzy nods, lowers her laptop cover. Pauses but doesn't break eye contact.

"Put Donna in the video. Just put her in. Put her in however you want."

Bev sits down again. Izzy unwraps the tiny blue chocolate ball and pops it into her mouth. Bev wishes she had taken one too but can't bring herself to reach for the dish now.

"We all have to put up with something," Izzy says.

"Excuse me?"

"That was Donna's line. *We all have to put up with something,*" says Izzy. She crushes the chocolate wrapper. "You don't remember, do you."

The knitters, all taught by Donna. Four or five of them working quietly with needles and wool for twenty-minute stretches on their lunch breaks. It was peaceful, the clicking of the needles as they created scarves and hats and sweaters. Separate, but together. Breaking the silence, Donna would blurt an observation or opinion or conclusion, nuggets they eventually christened *Donna's Random Purls*.

Bev swivels the chair, tippy-toed feet on the carpet.

"No, I didn't remember."

"But now you do."

"Yup."

"We do, don't we?"

"Yes."

Bev has weathered enough team meetings to know there's no debating a profit-sharing partner/litigator who owns a collection of $800 blazers for court days. Righteous indignation drains away, replaced by something she cannot yet identify.

Izzy picks another chocolate ball. This one, red-foiled, she flicks across to Bev, who stops it like a puck.

"Look, I'm the person trying to help you."

"I know."

"Good. I wonder, need to ask, what do you really want?"

AS SHE TRIES to travel home at the end of the day, Bev discovers that the plastic card that raises the steel gate to allow her to enter and exit the parking garage is not where it is supposed to be. It has disappeared from her car key pouch, so she is trapped. Bev leans through the car window and presses the intercom at the gate. It rings with no answer.

She tries again and a male voice says, "ParkRight." Bev tells him she's a monthly client, the lady from yesterday who told him about the illegal parkers.

"You gave me gum."

The intercom voice says, sorry, he is not that guy. He is speaking to her from the ParkRight call centre in Toronto and he tells her she must pay the maximum daily rate. Then the machine will pop out a receipt. Tomorrow, if she proves she's a monthly parker, the office will refund her money.

"It's the best I can do," he says.

The stranger's disembodied voice, two thousand kilometres away, though distorted by the metal box of the garage speaker, comes across as polite and respectful. He likely understands most people do not lie. But no matter, he has zero authority to raise the gate. There's no reason to blame him.

She almost replies that she won't be in tomorrow but she knows that isn't true. In just a couple of hours, she will be right back here, even arriving a few minutes early to replace her pass and claim the money she is owed. Then she will have to walk extra fast to get to work on time.

She digs out her credit card and slides it into the slot, enters her banking code to pay the same thirty-two dollars as everyone else who has lost their swipe card or misplaced a paper ticket. She waits for the gate to open. As soon as the barrier lifts, she accelerates and without checking for oncoming traffic, makes a sharp right turn onto the downtown street.

And then a taxi from out of nowhere.

It brakes hard and swerves to avoid a crash, the cabbie leaning on the horn. His gold Camry's front bumper just misses her rear end as she enters the street.

She pulls over, shaken, and the cab pulls alongside.

A man barely older than her sons extends his body toward his open passenger window. He screams into the space between their vehicles.

"What the fuck is the matter with you?"

"I didn't see—" she begins, but he isn't interested in her apology.

"Stupid bitch," the man yells.

She tries again.

"I'm sorry, I just—"

"Whatever," he interrupts. He slashes the air with his entire arm.

"Stupid, stupid bitch. Learn to drive."

He speeds away without closing his window.

Bev watches him disappear down the road that leads to the Halifax–Dartmouth bridge, gone as quickly as he appeared.

She tries to catch her breath. Needs to regain composure before starting afresh.

I'm fine, she tells herself. *It's all fine.*

But then she notices that her emergency bag has slipped off the passenger seat and the contents of her private desk drawer have spilled onto the filthy mud-caked rubber mats of her car. She takes stock. The travel mug, and her lip balm. The picture of the boys when they were young. And then these two women, friends, dressed up as pirates. Everything that matters is down there.

Train Stories, Abridged

THE CARDIOLOGISTS AND THE MEDICAL STUDENTS WHO TRAIL behind them on their daily rounds take turns asking Vera Vucovic, "Have you been under stress?"

In reply, there's always some version of "come on, life is stress" or "there must a sick person who needs this bed." She usually adds that she needs to get home to her rescue dog, Katya.

"She is now my responsibility, you understand."

Then one of Vera's three daughters chases the doctors down the corridor of the Halifax hospital to remind them, again, that Vera lost her husband—their father—just eleven months ago. If this isn't stress, what is? They want the physicians to consider the whole picture, the facts.

Despite her daughters' vigorous interventions, the doctors conclude Vera's heart attack is a mystery. They, the experts, have found nothing to fix. Though she is eighty-six, they detect no blocked arteries, no faulty valves, and no unusual heart rhythms. Science cannot provide a reason for what happened to Vera. Medicine, the cardiologist overseeing Vera's care explains to the three daughters, is both a science and an art.

"Sometimes there are more questions than answers," she says to the women one day in the hospital hallway. "After forty years at this, all I can tell you is there isn't always a clear diagnosis, even though we all want one."

Vera says she does not care about what happened or what might happen; the only thing on her mind is that Katya needs her. It was bad enough the dog had been abandoned to a stranger when Vera "collapsed"—she strongly disputes that description—on their morning walk. The stranger had found Vera lying on a bench, didn't believe she "was only resting," and called 911. Seeing Katya's sad, scared face as the paramedics loaded her into the ambulance was awful, Vera tells her granddaughter, Sadie, on one of their twice-daily calls.

"I had to leave her behind."

"You had no choice," says Sadie. "Under the circumstances."

Sadie has moved into her grandma's condo while she's in the hospital. She walks Katya before and after university classes. She carefully measures dog food and allows the creature to cuddle up next to her on the couch while she studies. Plays classical music on the kitchen radio all day, as instructed, because this is what Katya has become accustomed to in her nine months with Vera. Sadie phones her grandmother in the hospital every morning and evening and holds the phone to one of the dog's floppy ears so she can hear Vera's voice.

"Katya can't handle any more disruption," Vera announces on day four, even though Sadie insists the dog is fine. As soon as she has the energy, Vera rises from her hospital bed and agitates for discharge. She circles the halls of the cardiac care unit in her green hospital gown and blue striped robe. Untied, strings flapping, lobbying random nurses for liberation.

"Look. I'm walking. Sick people don't do this," she says.

Vera embarrasses her daughters the entire week. Argues, tries to convince nurses and doctors to take sides. She has been this way since her husband died. They wonder if the loss of their father peeled off a layer of restraint, or maybe the heart attack is a truth serum, but nothing the daughters do is right.

"They think I'm incompetent," Vera says to the chief cardiologist one day after her oldest daughter, Maria, Sadie's mother, butts in and answers medical questions on her behalf.

"You don't seem incompetent to me," the doctor says.

When they discharge Vera on day seven, she declares the faux health crisis over and shoos Sadie's aunts back to Toronto. They take her at her word that she doesn't need them; time for everyone to get back to daily life. Sadie's mother, Maria, returns to work but Sadie remains planted in the guestroom, fibs that she's having roommate problems.

"I'd appreciate the break," she tells her grandmother. "Maybe I can help walk the dog while you get settled."

"Sure," says Vera. "I don't mind."

On her first afternoon home, she stands guard on her condo balcony in a fluffy pink bathrobe while Sadie walks the dog on the trail below.

Vera cross-examines her granddaughter afterward.

"Did she poop?"

"A small one. I used the bag and put it in a garbage bin."

"You weren't gone very long. You followed our usual route like I told you?"

"Yes."

"You gave her treats?"

"Of course."

Vera crouches and holds Katya's face in her wrinkled hands. "Did you miss me?"

On her third day home from hospital, Vera puts on her favourite purple tracksuit and stuffs her ancient vinyl fanny pack with a vial of nitroglycerin, a handful of the dark chocolate squares she buys at Costco by the jug, a baggy of dog treats, poop bags, and her key fob.

"Let's go."

She leads Sadie and Katya to the one-kilometre gravel trail behind her building. The path loops behind a block of low-rise condos and apartment buildings and edges around a rocky point jutting into Halifax's Northwest Arm. They move slowly, and after a few minutes, Vera plunks on a bench and Katya sits on the ground in front of her.

"Don't tell your mother. She'll hire one of those old-people babysitters."

"I won't tell."

Sadie wonders if this is the same spot where the stranger found her grandmother sprawled, but doesn't ask. She joins Vera and accepts one of the tiny squares of chocolate. It's a sunny Saturday, warm for October, and there are sailboats to watch.

"School?"

"I like my history classes. Maybe that'll be my major," says Sadie, fiddling with the candy wrapper.

"History? What kind of history?"

"We're doing Europe right now. Wars mostly."

"Anything about us? Our war? Are you learning any of that?"

"What do you mean, Grandma?"

"Our family's war. The second one."

Katya is restless. She tugs on the leash.

"Oh, you want to explore," says Vera to the dog.

She presses a button to extend the tether. She and Sadie watch Katya pull away to a clump of trees. The dog's nose and paws investigate the rocks and dead leaves. And the scents, vestiges of domesticated and undomesticated animals that have left detectable traces.

Vera turns back to Sadie. "Nonna Marija. My mother. Your great-grandmother. She was in the Resistance."

"I didn't know that."

"So many people were. Why not our people?"

Katya paws pine needles, looking for buried treasure.

"Did your little friend across the hall pee there? Is there a mousie?"

"You know, she was a war hero," Vera continues. "She blew up a train bridge. Back in Yugoslavia. When there was a Yugoslavia."

"Really?"

Vera digs out some dog treats.

"Come to mama, Katya."

The dog knows there's no obligation or expectation to perform. She doesn't need to sit or beg or roll over or do anything special for Vera to give her a treat. None of that is necessary. All she needs to do is exist.

Katya eats out of Vera's palm while Sadie scratches the dog behind her soft ears.

"Well, she helped blow it up," says Vera. "A train bridge."

"Can you tell me?"

"Sure. I was maybe four?"

"And you remember?"

"I was four, maybe. I didn't know what was really going on, but Nonna Marija put me on a train with a strange man. Said it was a visit to my aunts. They lived in Rijeka, by the sea. She said it was a vacation and she would come soon. She put me on this train with a man I never saw before and gave us a basket of food. I remember he was tall and he held the basket. I don't know if he spoke to me but at some point he put the basket on my lap and told me to eat. And then he stood up, walked down the aisle, and through the door of the railcar."

The dog lays her head on the bench, between Sadie and Vera.

"The man never came back."

Sadie looks at her grandmother's face. She has amazing skin, given her age. Just a few creases around her eyes and some laugh lines.

"He left you? Alone?"

"It was different then."

"Still…"

"I kept very quiet. I didn't move. I held the basket tightly."

"Were you scared, Grandma?"

"I didn't eat any of the food," Vera says, eyes on Katya. "I looked out the window. It was grey and rainy. There was nothing but trees. So many trees."

Sadie lays her young hand on Vera's old hand but is not surprised when her grandmother gently dislodges her fingers to pat Sadie's forearm.

"At the station were my aunts to meet me," she continues. "It was dark I think."

"So, the man on the train," Sadie says. "The bridge."

"I didn't see or hear it but somewhere, we crossed a bridge. And after we crossed the bridge, this man blew it up behind us."

"Really?"

"Sure," says Vera. She pushes down with her palms to make it easier to get up from the bench.

"That fixed those Nazis. For a day or two, anyway."

"SHE NEVER TOLD me any of that. None of it. She tells me nothing," says Maria, who has just picked up Sadie at Vera's. They're on their way back to Sadie's apartment.

Maria's driving is worse than usual. She changes lanes on the Armdale Roundabout without shoulder checking and gets a horn blast from a pickup truck that swerves to avoid them. Agitation is her mother's go-to emotion these days, so Sadie buries her own anxiety under layers of surface calm. There's enough drama already.

Maria pulls over on a side street off Quinpool Road. She flicks on the flashing hazard lights and grills Sadie. If the bridge blew up, wouldn't Vera have heard a huge boom? You'd remember that, wouldn't you? When they arrived at the next station, wouldn't there have been a commotion, soldiers and sirens? How much dynamite can a rucksack hold anyway?

"God, you're so literal," says Sadie, who pictures a man using the child as a shield to avoid suspicion. He hops off the train along the way to join co-conspirators in a covert operation that could have unfolded days or even weeks later.

"Does it have to make actual sense to be true?" she says.

"This is a highly unlikely situation," Maria concludes. "Highly unlikely."

"I'm telling you the story she told me. I can't tell you what she left out," says Sadie.

"Come on," says Maria. "Who puts a little girl on a train, alone, with an underground operative?"

"Can you *please* just take me home?"

"You know, my mother and her mother never got along," continues Maria. "They bickered in Croatian, constantly. Who knows what it was all about."

Sadie settles in and closes her eyes, pictures herself in child's pose on her bedroom yoga mat.

"At Christmas, Mom would make a big fuss," her mother says. "She'd put up the tree in early December, bake and cook and stash all this food in the freezer. She always said 'all love goes through the stomach.'"

"Still does," says Sadie, opening her eyes and glancing sideways at her mother.

"Nonna Marija would show up at Christmas dinner in faded, baggy clothes. My mother would be furious. Why didn't she dress up a little, why didn't she even try? And when we all complimented the meal, Nonna would shrug. 'Too much,' she'd say, dismissing the table, the tree, and the gifts. So much work, gone in one wave."

Maria imitates her Nonna in the telling. Sadie recognizes the replica wave because she grew up with it. It's the same gesture Maria makes when she's impatient or annoyed. Her mother is unaware, Sadie supposes, of what has been inherited.

Genealogy is a tricky thing, she knows. Her father's parents each claim a clear line back to the first settler ship to arrive in Nova Scotia from Scotland, but Sadie has never seen proof. If every Nova Scotian insisting on *Hector* connections really had them, that was a crowded boat. The *Hector* story might be no more than a family myth, but even if it's true, Sadie thinks it's a strange thing to brag about.

On the other side, history has extinguished family lore. It has reduced their ancestors to a bundle of bare facts and vague maybes. Nonna Marija was a Slovenian Catholic. She married a Croatian Jew named Josip Goldstein and they settled in Zagreb. Vera was their only child, raised Catholic. The Nazis killed Josip in Dachau, along with his sister, brothers, mother, cousins, aunts, and uncles, likely also some great-aunts and great-uncles. Sadie doesn't know any of the names of these erased people. She wonders if her grandmother even knows. It's not something anyone in the family speaks about.

She looks across to her mother, who's now staring at the steering wheel, and says, "I remember her."

"You remember Nonna Marija?"

"I do."

"No you don't, not really," insists Maria, spraying the windshield with fluid and watching the wipers' futile attempt to clear bird poop. "She was in a nursing home, out of it. Who would take a toddler there?" she says.

But Sadie is firm, says she has flashes of memory. Images of a skinny old woman in raggedy clothes that hang from her bones. Her voice is high-pitched, grating. She lunges at Sadie, tries to grab her. Sadie buries her face in her mom's legs.

"Doubt it. Children can't form reliable memories at that age," Maria says, restarting the car and pulling out into the street without signalling.

But Sadie knows what she knows.

THE NEXT DAY, Sadie takes the bus to visit Vera and walk the dog with her. This time they make it a few hundred yards farther along the trail, to the next bench, before they rest.

"Progress. See?" says Vera, as she sits. The heart attack was bogus, she has decided, exaggerated by her daughters and the doctors.

Sadie sits next to her grandmother. "You can't just turn things into what you want, you know."

Vera laughs and hands her chocolate. "Why not?"

"That story about the war and the train and your mother, where was it? Where was this bridge? Maybe we can look it up."

"How would I know? Katya sweetie, poop *before* treats."

"How are you sure the bridge blew up? You didn't see it."

"Maybe my aunts talked about it." Vera zips up her fleece jacket against the early November chill. "I'm not sure how the story came."

Because her mother's voice is clanging in her head, Sadie is tempted to doubt.

"So Nonna Marija and this man were working together and their plan was that he would leave you alone on a train. Abandon you."

"It was different then, like I said. Not like now when you can't even send a kid for milk. Where was I going to go?"

The dog is at their feet, nuzzling her head into Vera's knees. Vera tells Katya how pretty she is and about the extra-special treat she'll give her at home, even though she's a naughty little girl who hasn't pooped yet.

AFTER THEY BURIED Sadie's grandfather, Miro, last year, they all crowded into the family cottage, a log home perched on a stony cliff on the Atlantic coast. They claimed spots on couches, bunk beds, floors, and futons while Vera slept alone in the main bedroom. Sadie's mother and aunts spent evenings on the screened porch drinking wine and eating bowls of chips and Cheezies. Their chatter rose and fell as Sadie tried to sleep on the living room sofa bed, surrounded by snoring cousins on the floor. Every evening after Vera went to bed, Sadie's aunts and her mother talked endlessly about their father.

How could they do without him? And how would Vera manage?

One night Sadie heard her own mother say, "When we were little, if there was thunder and lightning at night, when we were scared, he was the one we ran to. Him, not her. We never ran to her."

"Well, *she* slept like a log," an aunt said. The Ontario aunts had similar voices, so it was difficult to tell them apart.

"No. God no. She was scared shitless," said another aunt. "She hated the noise, the rumbling. You don't remember?"

OVER THE NEXT few weeks, Sadie visits Vera regularly. As they walk, a little farther each time around the gravel loop, her grandmother returns to the train story, over and over. Sadie deduces that her job is to listen, not question. With each telling, the details shift. Nonna Marija was at the train station in her best dress to see Vera off with kisses and tears. The basket contained bread and chocolate, which she happily enjoyed on the train. In another version, the man was a cousin, not a stranger. He came to the house; he had tea and took her to the station. The man was carrying a massive rucksack; the man carried nothing. He told her stories and sang songs on the train, or maybe he was stone silent until he disappeared. Her mother followed very quickly and they reunited at the seaside as promised. She did not immediately appear at the seaside, but vanished for a whole year. Or was it just a month or two?

Sadie prefers the stark, original version: Brave child, mother's sacrifice, heroic act of resistance. There's no need to embellish.

The common thread is that when Nonna Marija does reappear, no one explains her absence. They all remain in Rijeka, the three women raising Vera together. Vera still can't pinpoint how she came to learn about the bridge explosion. Maybe her aunts told her when she was older. But then again, it is possible, she theorizes, that she overheard it late one night as the aunts, and maybe even her mother, drank plum brandy.

"Shouldn't I remember better?" Vera asks Sadie one day. They're drinking tea after their walk and eating Danish butter cookies from bone china plates. Sadie has just admired Katya's new pink-flowered collar.

"Sometimes, very quick, I remember the thing I didn't remember," says Vera. "Then sometimes, also quick, I forget what I forgot."

The dog takes up most of the sofa, its head in Vera's lap. Family visitors know the couch is permanently reserved for the dog but it drives Sadie's mother crazy to sit on an uncomfortable rocking chair watching Katya lounge and drool on plush cushions.

Vera says, "Maybe she knew she was going into the camp."

"Camp," says Sadie. "Camp?"

The Ustaše, her grandmother says. Puppets for the Nazis. Sadie picks up her phone.

"What was the name of the camp, Grandma? I can look it up."

"No thank you dear," says Vera, sipping tea from a cup decorated with red roses and rimmed with gold. She loves pretty dishes and worries that none of the grandchildren will want them.

"My aunts," she says, putting down her cup. "One was a spinster with a lump in her back. Such beautiful soups she made. The other aunt was a kind of widow. Did the fiancé die in the war maybe? Maybe. Anyway, he was gone. The widow brushed my hair, braided my hair, put flowers in my hair."

Vera offers the plate to Sadie. Sadie doesn't like these sugary cookies very much but takes one.

"On sunny days we all swam in the sea," says Vera.

"TELL ME SOMETHING you've never told your mother," Vera says to Sadie one day as they circle the trail. They have played this game forever.

"A juicy one."

"Well, I guess I have a train story too," Sadie says after quickly eliminating 99 per cent of her other stories. It happened last year when she was backpacking in Europe with two girlfriends. After a few weeks on the road in France, they decided to travel to Lyon to stay with a girl they used to hang out with during their first year at Dalhousie. This girl, Emma, she was teaching English in a high school or maybe a college. Sadie wasn't sure. They weren't super close anymore, but Emma had a downtown apartment where they could all crash for a few days as they were passing through.

They took the high-speed train from Nice to Lyon. When they arrived at the Lyon train station, Sadie tells Vera, her two girlfriends pushed ahead, but Sadie hesitated.

"I didn't know how it worked, Grandma. That the train stops only for a few minutes, that you need to move quickly or else."

The aisle was crowded. She let an old couple with a beat-up suitcase pass. Next a couple with toddlers, and then the train doors slid shut. She did not make it through.

Vera shakes her head. "Ah. You were separated from your friends."

The train left the station, and she was trapped, Sadie explains. It didn't stop again until the Gare de Lyon in Paris.

"I ended up in the wrong Lyon," says Sadie.

"But a good Lyon, Sadie," says her grandmother with a smile. "And then?"

Then, Sadie says, she had to stay in a crowded hostel dorm room with strangers, a group of German girls.

"In the end, no big deal," Vera says. "You had a nice little adventure."

Sadie agrees yes, it was an adventure. The next morning the German girls invited her along, they all went to the top of the Eiffel Tower, and then she split off and spent the afternoon by herself at Musée d'Orsay.

"I never told Mom. You know how she is," says Sadie.

Vera seems pleased with the small, shared secret, stops walking, and turns to her. "The memory is the important thing. You keep a good memory always of this adventure."

—

THE GUY SITTING across from Sadie on the train has a pock-marked baby face, a shaved head, and a black leather wallet on a thick metal chain. The chain is attached to a studded black leather belt. He wears headphones and stares out the window with empty eyes. There is a bag of Haribo hard candy on the vacant seat beside him. His outfit—leather jacket, wool socks tucked into black jeans, heavy boots—looks odd on a warm June day.

He doesn't look at Sadie because she isn't there. Without her friends, she feels as if she has vanished, ceasing to exist when she hesitated and allowed everyone else off the train first. They knew what clueless Sadie didn't know: that the train will pause for only two minutes, that the automatic doors will shut no matter who is supposed to get off, even if your friends are pushy and maybe a bit rude and leave you behind, even if your ticket is for Lyon and not for Paris.

This train's job is to reach Paris in 117 minutes. No matter that your friends notice your WTF face in the window as the train leaves the station. They are only yards away, but it might as well be miles, and by the time you finally turn away, they have long since disappeared, replaced by backyards that whiz by in a blur.

Her new seat faces west and she can see the sun drop. Both the train and the sun move quickly, but Sadie sits tight and still as an invisible string pulls the train to Paris and the sun falls to the horizon. She needs to pee and worries her period is coming but there's no one to guard her luggage. Her friends are seasoned travellers with light back-packs. She brought a backpack too, but it is the type that converts into a rolling suitcase—too bulky for the train, she understands, too late. Signs plastered all over the train car threaten a fine of 200 euros for riding without a validated ticket. Should she tell the conductor, or hope he doesn't ask for her ticket? These things are random, she suspects, a mat-ter of bad luck. Sometimes the conductor comes by, some-times not.

A second guy joins the man-child. Skinny as a preteen, he also wears a leather jacket, jeans tucked into thick socks, boots. Same buzzed hair. He sits in the empty seat across from Sadie, grabs the bag of Haribo, shoves a candy into his mouth, and throws the wrapper on the floor. Then he pushes up his sleeve to show the other guy a tattoo on his hairless forearm. It is a black circle overlaid with a cross.

She wonders if it's a hate symbol but feels guilty for assuming these two people are what they appear to be. They are probably harmless.

Her friends text. They try to help. They tell her there's a hostel near the Gare de Lyon in Paris but the neighbourhood is sketchy.

"Don't walk alone. Uber," says one of them. "Taxi stand at station door. Don't walk," writes the other.

The pair sitting across from her stick out their tongues and laugh at each other's candy stains. One has a blue tongue, the other a green one that he wiggles like a lizard. Then they get up and the pockmarked one grabs his knapsack; his heavy boots stomp on Sadie's silver and white running shoe. When she flinches and says "ah!" no one looks her way. *I guess invisible people don't feel pain.*

She watches them through the glass door separating the train cars. They block the passageway where the bathroom is. They pass a liquor bottle and a vape pen back and forth until a ticket agent interrupts the party. His body language tells Sadie that they're being warned. The skinny one stands behind the agent, makes mocking faces only his buddy and Sadie can see. The ticket agent leaves the pair with a final finger wag.

The baby-faced one comes back alone, pulls out his phone, and gets back to work on the candy, sucking and crunching like a four-year-old.

The second guy disappears into the bathroom. Now Sadie really really needs to pee, but he doesn't emerge for a while. When he finally comes out and saunters to the next train car, she drags her ridiculous suitcase/backpack through the sliding doors, arriving at the same time as a woman in her forties. The woman has smooth, dark hair and a watercolour silk scarf looped around her neck.

Sadie allows the woman to go first, crossing her legs against the pressure of her bladder, hating herself for falling prey to the same courtesy or lack of nerve that left her abandoned in the first place. But as the woman opens the bathroom door to enter, she recoils and backs into Sadie, hitting her breast with an elbow.

The shattered glass of a liquor bottle is jammed into the toilet on top of a heap of shit. The stench is overwhelming.

Rolls of toilet paper, shredded like confetti, cover the floor, and fill the sink. On the bathroom mirror in green marker, a swastika, and *MANGE MA BITE, BAISSE TOI.*

The woman speaks quickly. Sadie can't keep up with her French. The woman flicks her hand as if to say "go" and Sadie picks up the word *controleur. The controleur...go get the controleur.* She pushes Sadie toward the sliding door.

"Non merci. I'll stay here. Je reste ici. I'll guard the door," Sadie says, a firm grip on her suitcase handle.

In the kerfuffle that follows, Sadie remains planted between the train cars. She doesn't return to her seat. Doesn't lug her heavy pack in search of a clean bathroom. Better to stay put, hold your pee, and be the first one out when the train pulls into the station.

———

SADIE SITS NEXT to her mother at the kitchen table. Maria wears reading glasses and peers into her laptop screen as if it's a glowing crystal ball. They've just finished supper and her dad is busy marking grade twelve history papers in the den.

Her mother has a mission: determine the truth of the alleged bridge sabotage. One of the many problems with Vera's train story/stories, as Maria sees it, is that Rijeka was heavily bombed during the period when Vera was supposedly cloistered there with her aunts.

"Bombarded," she says, pointing to the screen. "Look. The Germans, the Allies, everyone."

"So?" says Sadie, licking chocolate ice cream from her spoon.

"There was guerilla fighting. No place to send a child."

"I doubt there was a better option."

"What do you mean?"

Sadie puts down her spoon, pushes away her empty dessert bowl, and tells her mother about Nonna Marija and the camp. Immediately, her stomach cramps. This disclosure is unauthorized. It is a mistake, a betrayal. Not Sadie's story to tell. But it's too late because Maria is already tapping her keyboard.

"This is important to know," she says without looking up.

Maria does legal research for civil lawsuits and is an expert in the value of a lost limb, a lost livelihood, a lost future. Her methods are impeccable as she researches complex, serious matters on databases created for professionals. But for her own family story, she is impatient and relies on Google.

It takes Maria less than a minute to develop a theory about which camp it must have been. She turns the screen toward Sadie.

"Jasenovac," she announces. "The Auschwitz of the Balkans."

Sadie has done her own quiet internet rummaging. She has her own questions and potential answers, but says nothing. She moves her chair closer and peeks over her mother's shoulder as she scrolls through a short list of results. There isn't much to chose from in English.

Her mother clicks and falls into a photo archive. Sadie tripped into the same hole a few hours ago, and knows what's coming.

"This won't help Grandma," she warns as her mother flips through the image gallery that Sadie found this morning. The shots are grainy. Some are blurry.

Children, with and without mothers. No men except guards.

Maria puts a hand to her mouth. "Look," she says.

Sadie tries—and fails—to blink away a twitch in her left eye. Attempts to speak slowly, calmly. "What is the matter with you?"

Her mother's eyes move away from the screen, to her hands on the keyboard, and then to Sadie's face. "What's the matter with you?" she says. "Isn't this important work? Family work?"

She shakes her head and resumes clicking. "Look," she says again, this time pointing at the screen.

The person or local museum or historical society, whoever created this record—this crude, blunt-force evidence bank—couldn't or didn't make it fancy. Maybe they worried that time was running out as the people with the memories disappeared. The website looks like the school project of a kid in the nineties but the short, bold Helvetica captions that run across the black and white photos are in several languages.

Piano wire.
Butcher knife.
Zyclon B.

Sadie leans across and slams shut the cover of the laptop. She is not gentle. Her mother whips away her fingers just in time.

"Jesus H. Christ. You almost hurt me," she says, pushing back her chair so fast it scrapes on the hard tile. Eyes wide and mouth open. Staring at her daughter.

"Just stop," says Sadie. She can't believe how this is playing out, what she just did.

"Stop what?" Her mother looks mystified.

"You think she needs to see all that, Mom, really?"

"If she's sharing these stories with you, she must want to know the truth."

"Oh, please tell me you aren't jealous that she told me and not you," says Sadie. "Please, Mom."

Her mother picks up her laptop and rises from the table. She's heading to her bedroom, Sadie supposes, to finish what she started.

"I'm only trying to track down the truth," Maria says as she leaves the kitchen.

"Think about it," Sadie says to the back of her retreating mother's head. "Why now?"

WHEN SADIE ARRIVES at her grandmother's condo the next day, she finds Maria in the living room giving the rocking chair a workout, gripping a cup and saucer and eying the sleeping dog on the couch. Vera appears from the kitchen with a plate of gingersnaps.

"Now we have a party," she says and takes her place close to the dog, leaving room for Sadie on the couch.

"I've been thinking about Nonna Marija," Maria says, putting down her cup and reaching for a cookie.

"Have you," says Vera.

"Something I did once," Maria says. "It wasn't good."

"Oh, okay," says Vera, passing the cookies to Sadie. "This is a You Story."

"Yes, if that's all right."

"Sure sure."

Maria swallows a bite of cookie, stops rocking, and sits on her hands.

"I was maybe fourteen? I got on the bus at the mall with my girlfriends. I'd just bought new Levis with babysitting money. Then Nonna Marija gets on the bus with Sobeys bags. There are no seats and no one at the front offers her one. It's summer. A hot day. But she's wearing that old raincoat and those black rubber boots with the orange stripe, hanging onto a pole with one hand, trying to hold on to two or three paper bags with the other hand. Guarding another bag with her feet."

Maria starts rocking again, sock feet on Vera's plush area rug.

"No one else's grandmother looked like that. So I pretend I don't see her. I fiddle with my own shopping bag and my purse. Maybe I slap on some lip gloss. One of the girls nudges me, points at Nonna and laughs and I probably laugh too. I probably laugh. When our stop comes, I have walk to past her to get off the bus. I peek back as I walk away and Nonna is staring out the window, right at me."

Vera gestures to the kitchen. "Sadie sweetie. Maybe you make us all fresh tea."

Sadie doesn't move at first but her grandmother points to the kitchen and hands her the empty teapot.

Grandma Vera's kitchen has walls and is defiantly not open concept, even though most of the neighbours have knocked down their walls. Vera prefers it this way. No one, loved ones included, needs to witness her dirty dishes or the measuring, chopping, and frying that makes a family meal.

Sadie rinses the teapot, refills the kettle, plugs it in, and tries to eavesdrop. But for once, they have lowered their voices. There's murmuring, more murmuring, and then silence—Sadie's cue to return from temporary exile with a pot of properly steeped, hot tea and a third cup.

"Since it's story time, I'll tell you about a Christmas when I was little," Vera says after pouring the tea. "There's no Santa though."

It was sometime during the war, Vera thinks. Her father was gone of course; her mother took her to a Saint Nicholas party at the church. All the children hoped for candy, an orange, maybe a small toy. Saint Nicholas's robe was red and gold and he wore a bishop's hat. He called the children's names one by one, and each time he pulled gifts from a velvet sack. Waiting her turn, Vera was nervous with excitement and anticipation. Finally, the scarlet bishop called her name.

"He handed me a beautifully wrapped package, bigger than any of the packages for the other children. 'Open it carefully to save the ribbon,' my mother said, so I made my fingers move in slow motion. I was very proud to untie the package without tearing anything.

"Underneath all that fancy ribbon and tissue paper, no chocolate, no toy. A bundle of dirty twigs, remnants of brown leaves. I looked at my mother. I looked at Saint Nicholas. I remember his whiskers hanging over his lips. His mouth was open and I could see his teeth.

"And then my mother spoke, loud enough for everyone to hear: 'This is a punishment from Saint Nicholas because you are a bad girl who won't sit still. Who won't eat everything on your plate, who talks too much.'

"I cried, of course. I cried in front of all those other children, their parents, in front of Saint Nicholas.

"And then I remember this dressed-up man, just a normal man, but also Saint Nicholas. He says: 'No, no.'

"He is looking at me when he talks, looking at me, and not at my mother.

'There has been a terrible mistake,' he says. 'This is a terrible mistake.'

"He pulls an orange out from somewhere beneath his robes and he puts it in my hands.

'Here,' he says. 'Instead.'"

THE THREE WOMEN make their way along a crusher dust trail that loops around a shallow pond. The park is home to squirrels, one family of deer, mallards, and the occasional blue heron.

"Watch for tree roots," says Vera. "And stones."

The city park is a two-minute drive up a steep hill from Vera's condo. She has graduated from the short walks behind her apartment. That's okay for a morning stroll, but on a fine weekend afternoon this is so much better. She has invited her daughter and granddaughter to join her and Katya on a route she has not tackled since the fake-not-real heart attack. Vera's fuchsia lipstick, a gift from her daughter, coordinates with her windbreaker and the new, slip-on Sketchers they shopped for together. A smooth leather pouch has replaced the battered fanny pack and is slung over her shoulder, crossbody. In her ears, the plain gold hoops she has promised to Sadie "when the time comes but not now."

There isn't enough room for grandmother, mother, and daughter to walk side by side on the narrow path, so they take turns teaming up. Sometimes Vera and her daughter walk together, sometimes Vera and her granddaughter. Mostly though, Vera hikes a few steps ahead of the other two and focuses on Katya. The dog sniffs and paws everything in their path.

"She remembers her secret places," says Vera as the dog pulls away to climb over rocks and reach the pond. When Katya wades into the mucky water, Vera sits on a worn bench and beckons the others to join her.

"Something else about my mother," says Vera, watching the dog splash.

"Okay Mom," says Maria.

"Is this one true?" says Sadie.

"Funny girl," says Vera. "It was during the war. Or maybe after."

Vera and her mother, Nonna Marija, on a crowded train. The train car is hot and they must stand. It smells like sweat; grime and dust coat the windows. Her mother carries a cloth bag containing empty milk jugs, a radio, and a second bag. The journey is short but then they must walk a long country road to a farm.

"To walk that far, I must have been five or six," says Vera.

They reach a ramshackle farmhouse. The messy yard stinks, there's a chicken coop enclosed in rusty wire. Two skinny girls about Vera's age with filthy matted hair stare at her dress, which is plain, nothing special, but clean. Her mother has just let down the hem because Vera is growing.

The plan is to trade the radio for food. It is not a smooth transaction. The farmer first offers only a few eggs and a jug of milk. But Vera's mother wears him down, haggles and berates him until he agrees to a dozen eggs, several jugs of milk, fresh vegetables, and a chicken.

Her mother points out the hen she wants. This one, not that one, she specifies.

The farmer enters the chicken pen and returns with the fattest hen. Marija turns it upside down, pins back its wings. She lays the hen on a stained wooden block and holds it down as the farmer slams his knife through its neck. The bird twitches, convulses.

"Done," says the farmer.

Vera's mother puts the headless, bloody, still-feathered bird in the bag and they begin the long walk back to the station. She entrusts the potatoes and carrots to Vera. Vera will miss their kitchen radio but they have another one in the living room. She holds tight to the vegetable sack.

"And that's the end of the story," Vera says. "There must be more but that's all I have. So clear and then nothing else."

Maria says, "That's okay. It's enough."

Vera sighs. These sighs, Sadie knows, could mean many things. She doesn't analyze them. They could signal sorrow or perhaps fatigue. Maybe they're restorative pauses before Vera moves on to the next thing.

"My mother. She knew how things worked. How to negotiate."

"Yes, she did," Maria says.

Vera stands up. "So stiff. We should move," she says, and begins to march in place, raising and lowering her knees in a slow but steady rhythm.

"Come on, you two, too."

Her daughter nods and her granddaughter smiles, as Vera gestures for them both to get up.

"Katya stop!" she yells suddenly, breaking the morning serenity of the park.

The dog is wading out of the pond, not to Vera but toward a cluster of ducks. The duck family, a mother and six tiny ducklings, huddle together about thirty yards farther down the shoreline.

"Katya. You come back right now!"

This is the first time Sadie has seen Vera angry at the dog, the first yelling she has witnessed. This never happens. She looks to her mother, who stands but raises her palms to signal hands off.

"Back, Katya. Now," screams Vera.

Then the old woman starts striding quickly, her face flush, blood flowing. Her new purse bounces as she navigates the uneven, rocky shoreline.

She yells again, louder now:

"Leave the little ducks alone. Stop it, stop it. Let them be."

Extermination

WITH THE KIDS AT BASKETBALL, IT'S AN OPPORTUNE TIME TO fight about money, but neither of them has the energy or will to continue. Instead, Richie drives to the gym, or so he claims, and Marina makes a batch of smoothies for later, dumping blueberries, yogurt, and whey powder into the blender without measuring. The smoothies began as a weekend treat—her idea, her fault—but have morphed into another daily chore that no one notices but everyone expects. Only the frozen fruit varies.

From the moment her eyes opened much too early, due to their inadequate blackout drapes, it was "internet bundle" this and "grocery budget" that coming out of her husband's mouth. Then he yammered about the price of the winter coat and boots she'd bought on sale.

"Family funds, major purchases," he'd complained, as if she didn't also have a paycheque electronically deposited into their joint account twice a month.

Saturday has barely begun and she is already exhausted. *Crawl back into bed*, her body begs.

And then she discovers a mouse in her kitchen sink. She is about to rinse out the Vitamix pitcher and jumps back, startled, when she spies it. The thing skitters beneath her hands and circles the basin of the shiny sink as if it's an Indy racetrack. Marina doesn't think, just reacts. She grips the sixty-four-ounce glass pitcher in two hands, raises it above the sink, and brings it down hard and fast.

The creature disappears under the raised lip of the pitcher's base. A four-pointed blade inside the pitcher obscures her view but Marina can see splayed, scrawny legs through the clear glass. She places the pitcher on the counter, reaches for her reading glasses on the windowsill, and examines the specimen in her kitchen sink. Her corrected vision brings the mouse into sharp focus. She has a clear view of its beady eyes. Open, staring.

One tiny, hairless foot wriggles.

No choice now, can't let the thing suffer. This time she pauses, considers, adjusts the direction of attack, calculates where the bottom lip of the jug must land. Takes her time because this mouse isn't going anywhere.

Her aim is perfect. The bottom edge of the family-sized glass pitcher, it turns out, is an effective, bloodless, guillotine. It breaks the neck without puncturing the skin. There's a dent in the mouse's torso from the impact of the opposite edge, and all foot movement has ceased.

She realizes that her blender manoeuvre must have worked like one of those old-school, spring-loaded snappers.

"I'm the trap today, you little bastard," she says to the lifeless creature. "That's me."

She has always had a complicated relationship with mice.

———

MARINA AND IZZY were hungover when they toured the North End flat. The night before, they'd made the rounds on Argyle Street in downtown Halifax after Marina broke up with her boyfriend, Richie. Again.

"Hope the third time's a charm," Izzy had said, over egg rolls and chicken fried rice at two in the morning.

The apartment smelled like what it was—a dump where a trio of twenty-year-old males lived, and a fourth crashed on the couch. The guys had moved out but my goodness what they left behind: old socks, random dirty cutlery, donair remnants, congealed Kraft Dinner on mismatched plates in one of the bedrooms.

The landlord opened all the windows before they arrived, but it didn't help. You can't disguise the smell of unwashed, worn again, and still unwashed T-shirts. Of rotting garbage hanging in a plastic bag on a kitchen doorknob. The aroma of nocturnal activities, solo and duo, hung in the air.

Joey, the landlord, was a cousin of a friend. The rent paid his mortgage. He wasn't much older than Marina and Izzy. It was the Labour Day weekend and they needed an apartment before the fall term. Joey told them the flat was empty but not yet cleaned. If they wanted to see it before anyone else, this was the time.

"Great location, lots of potential," said Joey, wannabe real estate mogul. Izzy liked that the bedrooms were about equal size, so no disputes over who got what. Marina liked the natural light streaming into the living room, sun dappling the maple floor.

But Jesus the stench. She thought she would puke.

"Smells like something died in here," she said.

Joey promised he'd scrub out the flat and they could move in next weekend.

"You better," said Izzy, and suggested they go to a nearby tavern to sign the lease.

On moving day, Marina carried a box of her mother's old pots and dishes into the kitchen. The stovetop was filthy. Joey or whatever cut-rate cleaner he hired had shoved tinfoil covers onto burners that were blackened with grease and baked-on food. She opened the oven door. Looked like chunks of charcoal. Had those guys dumped the remains of a hibachi? She poked the blackened bits and looked more closely. Charred fur. A tail. More fur, more tails. She slammed it shut. Tried to yell but it came out as a squeak.

"Izzy. Izzy. Izzy."

Marina found her in the driveway unloading a box of books, and dragged her into the kitchen.

"What's the panic?"

Marina pointed to the stove. Her friend opened the oven door, peered into the darkness.

"Gross," said Izzy and shoved her head in to get a closer look. "Where's that box with my rubber gloves?"

"Do you not see what I see?" said Marina.

"Good idea. We should take a picture." Izzy was going into second-year law school. "We can get a rent cut from that asshole. Breach of contract."

"Screw this," said Marina. "I'm out."

"Don't be such a baby," said Izzy. "Where's my Polaroid?"

Marina slept in her old twin bed at her parents' place that night. She sat on her floral bedspread and read magazines, permitted her mother to serve her grilled cheese with tomato soup for supper. After her parents went to bed, Marina went to the corner store, where she bought a large bag of ripple chips, a jar of onion dip, a pint of chocolate ice cream, and a family-size bag of Skittles. When she got home, she changed into pyjamas and set herself up in the den. She rearranged the couch cushions to make a backrest and settled in to watch *The Tonight Show* and *Letterman*, working her way through first the chips and candy, then the ice cream. Salty, sweet, crunchy, creamy. When she was done, she stuffed the empty packages into her knapsack and shoved it in her closet.

Izzy phoned a few days later with news. She'd crafted a letter to Joey that included the phrase "incinerated vermin." The letter helped her negotiate a rent cut of $120 a month, plus a visit from a pest control company.

"My advice? Just see this through. We'll have fun."

Marina could hear the living room TV blare downstairs as her parents watched the late news on CBC. They were either going deaf or making themselves deaf.

"Remember, your name is on the lease, with mine," said Izzy. "It's a legally binding document."

———

MARINA STARTED TO bleed in the pre-dawn hours of day five of her honeymoon. The cramps woke her up with a pain that rumbled like distant thunder, and then closed in at regular intervals. They were staying at a bed and breakfast in Lévis, taking a twelve-minute ferry ride across the St. Lawrence River to Quebec City every day to save on hotel costs. The breakfast of croissant and cappuccino that Marina had imagined turned out to be plastic-wrapped cheese slices on factory bread, with warmish coffee. She couldn't sort out if the problem was her unrealistic expectations or the breakfast itself. What should you expect for forty bucks a night?

The room was so tiny that their bed was pushed up against the wall. A scratched maple chest of drawers blocked the bottom of the bed so she had to climb over her husband to get to the bathroom. Richie didn't wake up. He was a heavy sleeper.

The bathroom floor was covered in black and white octagonal tiles. Marina peeled off the red lace panties from her wedding shower and sat on the toilet. She leaned over, held herself in her arms, and studied the pattern of the floor.

This bathroom window must face east, thought Marina a few hours later, as she watched the sun rise. How long would it be before Richie woke and noticed she wasn't lying next to him?

The pain finally drove her into the bedroom. She turned on the harsh overhead light and nudged her new husband.

"We need to get to the hospital."

"THIS IS NATURE'S WAY," said the doctor with a kind, sad smile as the sun set that evening. His English was impeccable and there was nothing to criticize about the treatment they gave Marina. She was numb from the waist down, drowsy with mild sedation. It was considered a minor procedure, so she was free to leave after a few hours in a recovery bed. They sent Richie and Marina on their way with a prescription for Tylenol with codeine. The doctor told them it was safe to travel but take it easy and watch for signs of infection. Marina assumed they would drive straight home to Halifax. She wanted to sleep in her own bed. Richie assumed they would continue the road trip to see the Expos. The compromise was two nights at the Château Frontenac with room service before they started for Montreal.

"It'll cheer you up," he said. He held her hand on chemin Sainte-Foy as they left old Quebec, his palm rubbing against her wedding ring.

They decided not to phone their parents. They hadn't told anyone about the baby in the first place.

THEIR STUDIO APARTMENT—billed as a "junior one-bedroom"—seemed to be just as they had left it. It was on the second floor of a building in downtown Halifax. The sleeping area was on the left when you came in the front door; there was a kitchenette and bathroom to the right, and two steps down to a sunken living room. A picture window overlooked a green space across from the Public Gardens. There was a pancake restaurant on the main floor where senior citizens and red-eyed students congregated. Richie could walk to the engineering firm where he was interning, and Marina could walk to the newspaper. An apartment for adults, Marina told Izzy.

Richie started unpacking as soon as they got in the door. Marina found a beer in the fridge and put her bare feet up on the new leather couch. They'd picked it together, spending two Saturday afternoons at furniture stores. The couch and matching chair were a gift from Richie's parents when they'd skipped a big wedding and had a family-and-close-friends-only dinner in a private room at a steakhouse.

Out of the corner of her eye, Marina noticed a flash of movement across the living room carpet.

"Did you see that?"

"See what?"

"Nothing."

She went back to staring out the window. Richie was sorting their dirty clothes into laundry loads.

"Sit with me," she said a few minutes later. "Come on. It's not like we're putting it in tonight."

Richie said he was almost finished.

"This is called *helping*. You don't want to spend your last day of vacation washing clothes."

"I wasn't planning to. Am I supposed to?" she said, sitting up now. Feet on the floor.

She felt the slightest pressure on her ankle. Felt it, then saw it. A pink, two-inch alien with a tail. It raced across the floor and disappeared under an armchair. Another one ran through her legs and followed the first. Then a third materialized in front of her, moved across the floor, hit the wall, and raced along it. A fourth or was it a fifth or was it the first again darted from under the chair and headed straight for her.

Hairless. Tiny. Everywhere. Marina climbed onto the sofa. Richie was separating cottons from knits when she screamed.

"What now?" he said.

She jumped off the couch and ran past him, hyperventilating down the hallway to Gary the super's apartment and banged on his door. When he opened, she couldn't get the words out. Had to choose between speaking and breathing.

"Mice," she finally said.

They moved in with Marina's parents for a few weeks. She never entered their old apartment again. Refused to set foot in it even though Gary brought in an exterminator. The exterminator said the mother mouse likely came in under the apartment door. She used old newspapers to make a nest under the fridge, gave birth there.

"Bad timing," said the exterminator.

"We're clean people," said Richie.

"Nothing wrong with you," the exterminator said, as he was obliged to say to all infested clients. "Probably the pancake place downstairs. The apartment was empty and seemed safe to her is all."

Izzy offered to write a letter to the property manager to get them out of their lease but that wasn't necessary. The building attracted young professionals who wanted to live downtown. The owners didn't want rodent stories to get around, for the mice to be exaggerated into rats, or for a single nest to be gossiped into an infestation. Besides, Gary liked Marina and Richie, especially Marina. He was a fixture at the front door every morning, having a smoke as she left for work, and stationed there again when she came home at the end of the day. Always wanting to chat, telling her he liked what she was wearing, asking her what they were up to for the weekend. Borderline icky, Marina told Richie, but Richie said take it as a compliment. "He's like that with all the good-looking women in the building."

Gary put in a good word and the company offered Marina and Richie a bigger apartment on the eighth floor at the same rent.

"Take the deal," Izzy advised, and they did.

The new apartment had a proper separate bedroom and a view of the Public Gardens. Richie was content, but the place was never the same for Marina. For him, the apartment was a step up. For her, the whole building was tainted. She was wary; there must be rodents here, maybe undetected, but somewhere.

What stands out for her from that time is the Dairy Queen that was across the street from their building. The summer they married, DQ came out with the Blizzard. Whenever Richie worked late, Marina crossed the green area in front of the apartment and tried out a new flavour combination. She liked to eat on a bench in the Public Gardens, tucked in next to the flower beds. Dipping the red plastic spoon slowly into melting ice cream until there was nothing left. There was always a garbage can to get rid of the empty cup, and a bathroom nearby to wash the sticky residue off her hands. She worked her way down the list: Strawberry Cheesecake, Oreo, Choco-Cherry Love.

—

SHE LOOKS AT the carcass in her kitchen sink, worries the tail is suspiciously long. Richie and the boys aren't home yet, so Marina handles the rodent forensics. She remembers reading up on mice when she was younger, but maybe it's time for a refresher. She turns on the iPad, types in *mouse versus baby rat*. Pictures and charts pop up.

She roots around in the front closet to find the arts and crafts box from when the kids were little. Good—they still have fragments of Bristol board. She positions a piece of blue cardboard on the living room floor and searches the junk drawer in the kitchen for the barbecue tongs. She can't find the tongs so makes do with two soup spoons, balancing the corpse between them and moving slowly so she doesn't drop it. She plunks the carcass on the cardboard, where the morning sun illuminates its brown and grey fur.

She'll need to measure the body and tail, she decides, and heads back to the arts and crafts box for a ruler. The wooden ruler has a sharp edge to make straight lines and a numbered edge for measuring. *Property of Jacob N.* is scrawled in red marker along the front.

Marina uses one of the spoons to nudge the body against the ruler. She pokes the tail to straighten it. It measures three inches, a vote for mouse.

Body length is four inches. A bit long for a mouse.

Furry tail, not bald and scaly. Mouse.

Ears, hard to tell given the creature's current condition. The chart tells her mice have bigger, floppy ears while rats have smaller ears and a bigger head. But this specimen has a broken neck and a crushed torso, so its proportions might be skewed.

Probably a mouse, not a baby rat. Probably. She can't be sure. She snaps a picture with her phone and texts it to Izzy.

"Looks suspicious," Izzy replies immediately.

Izzy is permanently suspicious, Marina thinks.

"Better check with an expert," her friend writes.

YOU KNOW WHAT they say about mice: there's never just one. Even if you don't see them or hear them, there are always others—somewhere in your home. They squeeze through tiny cracks and holes. They take advantage of weaknesses and flaws in your structure. That imperceptible opening where the electrical panel in your garage welcomes a thin wire into the wall of the main house, for instance. A rodent uses its sharp teeth to widen the space, and then it compresses and flattens its body thanks to a collapsible ribcage. If the mouse's head can push through, the rest will follow.

The mouse slides into your walls via the electrical panel, and then it runs that shiny copper wiring like the Yellow Brick Road through the walls until its rodent instincts lead it to the back of your built-in dishwasher, where a slight gap the lazy installers left behind is an open door.

Your kitchen. This is as good a place as any to nest. The first mouse shows the trail to others. They aren't too fussy about who they mate with, so when you take the kids skiing at Sugarloaf on March break, that's an opportunity to love the one they're with and expand their domain.

There is never just one mouse.

"I thought I heard something in the walls, but I ignored it," Marina tells the exterminator on a Monday morning two weeks later, the first appointment available in a busy mouse season.

"You didn't want to know," he answers. "People never want to know."

The exterminator is in his twenties, bald, and wears a navy cotton jumpsuit with Cory embroidered in cursive writing on a breast pocket. He balances a flashlight, phone, and clipboard.

The company's website had pictures of glowing young families standing in front of pristine homes. Cory explains that for mice, they give a three-month guarantee. He can seal openings and cracks, lay down traps and poison today, and come back in a few days to check things out.

But rats are something else.

"For that, we'd need a plan," he says.

A mouse, mice, or even a colony of mice, this Marina can cope with. She's not afraid but vigilance is required. And poison, as Cory said.

Poison, traps, vigilance.

But rats...

"Let's get started," the exterminator says. "Basement to attic."

"Can I show you something first?"

He shrugs.

The rodent carcass is in a freezer bag. Marina quarantined it in a corner of the chest freezer in the garage, after carefully reorganizing the Pizza Pockets, fries, plastic containers of homemade lasagna and chili, frozen fruit and vegetables, and the six chickens she'd bought on sale. She pulls on her blue rubber cleaning gloves and lifts the frozen hunk from the darkest corner of the freezer. She holds the bag flat across her palms and extends her arms to Cory.

"What do you think?"

He looks across at the frozen, dead rodent that his new client holds in her outstretched hands. He steps back for a second, then leans over.

"That's…you kept it?"

He waves off her offer to take the bag.

"You don't want to see it up close?"

Cory shakes his head, peering from two feet away at the ice crystals that cloud the plastic.

"Well," he says, "that is something."

An hour later, Marina and Cory drag the fridge into the middle of the kitchen. This is the final step in the house inspection. She can't remember the last time anyone looked under the fridge, let alone cleaned.

The floor is covered in debris. It looks like someone spilled a bag of loose tea or black rice. The droppings cover a forgotten photo that had strayed, unnoticed, under the fridge. A photo of their boys as toddlers. It used to be on the fridge door, secured for years under a magnet from a plumbing company. It must have slipped off the stainless steel, mislaid and unobserved for who knows how long. Rodent excrement now speckles the faded candy canes and elves on the boys' Christmas pyjamas, obscures their tiny preschool faces. These children could be anyone's kids.

The exterminator reaches down but Marina moves more quickly than the young man.

"I'll get that," she says. Still wearing her rubber gloves, she grabs the picture from the floor and stuffs it into the deep pocket of her grey cardigan.

The Marshmallow Contest

THEIR BATHROOM FAN IS TOO WEAK TO CLEAR THE AIR, SO THE foundation melts on her cheeks even as she sponges it on. The air conditioning is broken again.

Maureen Sullivan attempts to salvage her face. Tries a dusting of powder, only to see the fine grains settle in cracks and enlarged pores. She blots but the residue is a damp, spongy mess of sheer beige cream and neutral finishing powder. No time to start all over again. This will have to do.

Late September—hurricane season on the East Coast. Weather gurus are eying a tropical depression swirling in the Caribbean. The humidex is thirty-eight degrees with an 80 per cent chance of thunderstorms. Corporate golf tournaments, however, are never cancelled on a forecast. There is just one day, and it has been circled on the calendar for months. You show up, you honour your commitment.

Jim yells from the kitchen to get a move on. Maureen squints into the mirror, dabs her nose and cheeks one final time with the blotting paper, and joins him downstairs, where he stands at the breakfast bar jiggling his keys. The stale kitchen air surrounds them like musty velvet curtains.

Jim's *Sullivan Insurance* mug, stained with years of coffee, and his wet cereal bowl rest on the stack of legal paperwork and junk mail that clutters their grey granite countertop.

"We'll deal with—all of that—later," Maureen says. "Better go."

COASTAL GLEN IS a suburban Halifax golf course that winds in and out of ribbons of newish homes backing onto sloping greens. The Drive the Marshmallow contest is on the eighth hole, which has a manicured fairway running along a narrow strip of trees on one side, and a shallow, man-made pond on the other. It's a tricky hole.

The Sullivans set up their canopy and table just behind the tee. They wear logoed, polyester tournament shirts. It is an unfortunate, low-tech fibre that clings to damp skin. A sweaty Jim unfurls a ten-foot vinyl banner and is struggling to string it between two canopy anchors when a course official pulls up in a shaded golf cart. She looks to be in her late twenties and wears a club visor with a ponytail swinging from the hole in the back. As soon as she spies their setup, she shakes her head, ponytail bouncing.

"Banners are a level of recognition we reserve for platinum and gold sponsors. And of course, our major sponsor, AtlanticAssure."

AtlanticAssure.

Maureen works at a neutral expression. Sees her husband's rosacea deepen to crimson on the spidery veins of his nose and cheeks.

Tapping her white Coastal Glen stylus on a seven-inch tablet, the official reads, "Sullivan Insurance. Hole sponsor, $750, yes?"

"Come on," Jim says, pointing to their banner. "Not hurting anyone."

The official taps her screen. "Entitled to: easel sign, verbal recognition. One-inch logo on back page of tournament program."

Jim's damp, red face flushes even more. He says, "Of course, of course."

The club official pulls a metal easel and eighteen-inch-square sign from the cart.

"There," she says after setting them up and correcting a wobble on one of the easel's legs. "See? Your company logo is in colour. That's new for this year for our entry-level sponsors."

"Thanks for that," says Maureen.

The young woman climbs back into her cart and gives them a thumbs up.

"Breathe," Maureen says when the official is out of ear-shot, as she rolls up the Sullivan Insurance banner.

"Screwed over," says Jim. "Right out of the gate."

"Well, you knew the odds," says his wife. "Didn't you?"

THE GOLF SPONSORSHIP idea was born six months ago. The Sullivans enjoyed their new deck on a warm Sunday evening in early May, relaxing into the striped cushions of matching recliners. The leaves of the red maple hanging over the deck had just popped. After an endless cycle of stop-and-start construction, including, they agreed, stretches of completely unacceptable inactivity, their tri-level deck was finally finished. All their worries and complaints about how contractors neglect small jobs were forgotten and forgiven.

Their Maggie had just landed a full-time nursing job in Calgary. Officially launched. They agreed they needed a new project for this new phase. But the insurance business they grew up in had changed. Local companies had modernized, digitized, merged with other small players. Growth appeared to be the only option. They would focus on the booming Atlantic construction industry.

"We're poised to make the leap," Jim had announced to their employees at a weekly sales meeting.

Jim thought a corporate sponsorship at the construction association's autumn golf tournament was the perfect fit for their new marketing plan. He wanted to go big, be a marquee sponsor. It would cost $9,500. He visualized hosting the closing barbecue, saw himself presenting trophies. He would make a speech about how the Sullivans had sustained their independent brokerage, how they had survived while multinational companies and chains swallowed up small firms, how that made them the obvious choice for their clients' own burgeoning businesses.

Maureen, who did the books and knew how much cash was coming and going, had weighed it out and was partial to a cheaper option. "How about the Marshmallow Challenge?" she said after scrolling to the bottom of the sponsorship website on her phone.

"What?"

"Apparently, golfers will pay good money to see how far they can drive a marshmallow off a tee."

"Oh, that."

"$750," his wife said. "Proceeds to the new hospice."

Jim and Maureen discussed the pros and cons over their salad, steak, and merlot. When they sold insurance to a small business, they often talked about risk management. Consider the bad things that could happen—fire, flood, identity theft, computer viruses, lawsuits—and protect what you have. You must balance impulse with prudence.

The numbers proved that peril was always a statistical possibility.

"I think...the marshmallow hole," said Maureen.

Jim chewed a hunk of sirloin. "So that's where we're at?"

"For charity."

The pair sat quietly until interrupted by the drone of a

neighbour's lawn mower, followed by another and another, a symphony to mark the first grass cutting of the year.

"I need to get at that strip mall proposal," said Jim. "We need it."

His wife poured the dregs of the bottle into her glass. She had planned to tackle the invoices tonight but wasn't inclined to move. The new cushioned recliners were so comfortable and the deck reminded her of a Pinterest post, unsoiled, so far, with that green mossy scum that inevitably sprouts on wooden surfaces near the seacoast.

She was content to take it all in.

TOURNAMENT PLAY IS painfully slow. Inexperienced golfers dither and then apologize for holding things up. The course's infamous water hazards are an insect breeding ground. Windless air allows mosquitoes to form a ruthless flying corps that attacks in endless waves. People smart enough to have bug spray in their golf bags discover it makes an oily mess when mixed with sunscreen. The caterer has messed up the box lunches, so vegetarians peel ham off warm sand-wiches or throw them in the garbage and search their bags for plant-based protein bars. Meat eaters wonder aloud how hummus and iceberg lettuce with shredded carrots, slapped between two slices of bread, qualifies as a meal.

It's a scramble tournament with assigned teams of four. They all tee off, and the team's best shot is everyone's new starting point, so that even the worst player gets a fresh start. And so it continues, hole by hole, with equal playing time for all. It's supposed to be fun, it should have been fun, but it isn't. Maybe it's the weather, but there's a sense of drudgery as golfers steer electric carts along the gentle slopes of the course.

Jim plays with Amber, one of their best young sales-people, while Maureen and Tristan, another top seller, are stationed at the marshmallow contest hole.

Running the contest is tedious in the oppressive weather. They labour to keep things light and fun, bantering with each foursome that passes through. They store the marshmallows in a cooler with frozen gel packs. The gel packs keep them intact, maintain their basic shape, but are no match for the hot, moist air that squeezes from all directions. Marshmallow goo leaves a nasty residue on their fingers. They hadn't thought to bring wet wipes.

The minimum contest donation is ten dollars; most golf-ers pay twenty-five or fifty to hit a marshmallow or two—nobody wants to be labelled a cheapskate—and many crack inane jokes as they take their turn—nobody wants to be a poor sport. Maureen dutifully laughs at their self-depreca-tion, hands out marshmallows, and collects cash while Tristan measures their shots.

"How did you get stuck here?" he asks during a lull. He has just moved a red marker a few yards down the fairway to mark the longest marshmallow shot so far.

"It was a joint decision."

"Right. So how did I get stuck here?"

"Well, bit of a mystery...let's think on it a bit."

Jim and Amber drive up to the hole. He's behind the wheel, shouldn't be, Maureen immediately sees, and swerves too close to the easel, almost cutting off a cart carrying the rest of their foursome, two men in their thirties decked out in AtlanticAssure gear instead of tournament shirts.

"Shit," whispers Tristan to Maureen. "Look who they ended up with."

Jim does not look well. Sweat pours from his cap band, soaking his eyebrows and dripping into his eyes. But Amber appears unbothered, seemingly equipped with an internal thermostat set to cool. She is in her midthirties. A natural seller, Jim has said. She had taken up golf after he advised her it was a good way to meet potential clients. Amber said no thank you to his invitations—such kind and generous offers, she repeated every time—to practice with him.

Instead, she developed a passion for Zen golf. She signed up for a virtual clinic and then went it alone with YouTube and a phone app. In the office's tiny lunchroom, she had explained to Maureen and the others how Zen golf is based on Buddhist teachings. How important it is to remain in the moment and not worry about your score. This, she said, is the key to mental mastery, and mastery of the game.

"We produce what we fear," was her current favourite phrase, which on some days Maureen thought was utter bullshit but on others, spot on.

THE ATLANTICASSURE DUO, both in their twenties, take respectable marshmallow shots but land well behind the leader. They each put a ten-dollar bill in the jar.

Tristan pulls out beers for Jim and Amber from a cooler bag.

"Can't drink on duty," she says. "Water please."

"Amber. Let's do this," says Jim after downing half the bottle of beer. "Me first."

Maureen points to the cooler where they store the marshmallows, and he digs around. "Hey buddy, no need to poke them all," says one of the younger men, nudging his friend.

Jim finally shoves his chosen marshmallow onto the tee. He pulls his new driver, a Stealth Two Plus, delivered yesterday, from his golf bag. When Maureen had questioned the surprise charge on their company Amex—$1,113 with tax and shipping—he showed her the booklet it came with. It promised "the redistribution of mass for more forgiveness and stability," thanks to an adjustable sliding weight on the head that was billed as an "inertia generator."

"Oh please," she'd said.

Jim stands over the marshmallow, legs shoulder width apart, knees slightly bent. He rests lightly on the balls of his feet. He eyes the white mass of sugar, air, and gelatin below him. Maureen has no clue how to swing a golf club but notices that his grip is tight, making sharp, bony mounds of his knuckles. Jim rotates his torso, stiffly it seems to Maureen, swings the club over his head and then swiftly and smoothly connects with the target.

They all look to the sky, and then toward the fairway, but see nothing. The marshmallow clings to the club's brand new, scarlet face like lumpy, sugary mashed potato.

"Oh," says Tristan.

"Nice try, Jimbo," says one of the AtlanticAssure golfers, Matt or Chad. They'd introduced themselves but Maureen hadn't taken it in. Everyone on the golf course under thirty is a Matt or a Chad.

Jim takes a dry towel from his golf bag to clean the club but it's useless. The goo is a magnet for towel lint. Maureen hands him her water bottle to rinse it off.

"Good enough for now," she says. "We'll sort it out later."

Amber drinks from her water bottle and passes it back to Tristan as he hands her a marshmallow. She carefully places it onto the tee. Gets into position, rolls her shoulders back, and takes a few graceful practice swings. When she swings for real, the gluey marshmallow sticks to her driver for a second and then flops off the edge of the club just ten yards off the tee.

"Oops," one of the waiting golfers says and she shrugs.

"Again," says Jim, reaching into the cooler. "You need a better specimen."

Maureen rattles the jar of charity cash. "Pay up. That will be a second donation, folks, and you haven't even made your first."

Her husband produces a crisp fifty-dollar bill from his wallet and stuffs it into the jar.

"This is for both of us," he says and picks a new marshmallow.

"Try your seven-iron this time, Amber," he says.

Amber pulls the club from her bag. She murmurs, "Trust your swing." After one fluid move, the marshmallow arcs down the fairway. The other golfers hoot their approval. Tristan takes Amber's hand, raises their arms in victory and uses his phone to record the distance. It surpasses Chad and Matt's yardage, has landed just three inches short of the front runner.

"See what great coaching can do?" says Jim.

Matt and Chad laugh. "Sure, buddy, that must be it," one of them says.

Tristan hands Amber her water, lays his palms on her shoulders, and kisses her lightly on the lips. "I submit to Zen golf's ancient teachings," he says.

Maureen watches Jim watch Amber and Tristan. Everyone in the office except Jim knows they're a couple. It's bound to cause problems, but Maureen has decided it's none of her concern.

"Not my circus," she'd told herself. "Not anymore."

She looks to Jim. He's already in the cart, behind the wheel, beer in hand.

"Amber, we're holding up play. Let's go," he says.

"Not yet. We're still supposed to play the hole." She

reaches into her pocket for a ball and begins the twenty-five-yard walk to the forward tee that some people still call the ladies' tee.

"Hey, forward tee goes last," yells one of the AtlanticAssure guys.

"Let it go," says the other. "Doesn't matter."

Amber arrives at the forward tee, performs her swing ritual, and drives her ball down the middle of the fairway.

"There," she says after she walks back.

It's Jim's turn. He uses his new driver again, which is still sticky. At first things look good, with his ball flying high and far. But then it slices to the right.

"Oh no, Jimmy. Not the pond."

"I don't need a frickin' play-by-play," Jim says. Sweat stains gather at the crotch of his cotton shorts. Maureen wishes she'd suggested the black pair instead of the tan.

"Easy, buddy. No worries. One of us will get 'er done."

Jim shoves his driver back in his bag and takes the wheel again. Amber is barely seated, waving goodbye, when he pulls away.

"Jesus. That guy. Didn't wait for us," says one of the other golfers, laying down his tee and ball.

"Matt buddy, chill. Hold on. They aren't even out of range yet," says the person that Maureen will remember as Chad. "Don't want to thump 'em."

AFTER MATT AND Chad each drive their ball a few hundred yards down the fairway, high-five each other, and speed off, only the mosquitoes linger in the still air.

"You're getting bitten to death," Tristan tells Maureen, brushing away six or seven bugs feeding on her right forearm.

"Jesus, it's like they're swarming you."

Bleeding, swollen bites blanket her ankles, calves, thighs, her hands, and arms. Maureen looks down at her body like it belongs to someone else, someone who can't or won't stop scratching and picking until she bleeds. She finds a bottle of bug spray in her knapsack and hands it to Tristan. She holds her bare arms out from her body.

"Please," she says. "Easier if someone else takes care of it."

"This won't do," he says, handing the bottle back. He pulls out a can from his own bag. "Serious DEET is what we need."

She closes her eyes. After he sprays her arms, she lifts her hair and he coats the nape of her neck. She twirls slowly so he can cover the front and back of her legs.

"This weather," Maureen says. "Why don't the skies just explode already?"

THERE'S NO BREAK from the crushing mugginess. Iron-grey clouds bear down until the closing barbecue.

The clubhouse looks like an oversized suburban bungalow, with a wide deck along its length where a grill, buffet, and makeshift bar are set up. Golfers who had been eaten alive all day now line up to grab meat, to fill plates with blobs and clumps of nameless salads. No one sticks around on the bug-infested deck. The sponsor reps from AtlanticAssure rush people through the queue. Young men and women wearing fresh aprons with navy blue, stylized anchor logos distribute beef and bun as a finely-tuned production line. Thanks for coming out today, thanks for supporting community health care. Condiments and more beverages are inside. No one minds being herded. They hurry into the air-conditioned clubhouse.

Maureen and Tristan find Jim and Amber sitting side by side at an otherwise empty table at the back of the room.

"Why so pleased with yourselves?" says Jim. Tristan explains they've just taken photos with the marshmallow contest winner—a plumber—and the hospice director.

"They already tweeted it," says Maureen, pulling out her phone to show them.

"Looking good, Maureen," says Amber, who nurses a soda water, hair pulled up in a tidy bun. She picks at a green salad with chickpeas.

"I put it on Insta," says Tristan.

"That was supposed to be me," says Jim. "We decided."

"Couldn't wait," Maureen says, sitting across from her husband. "Things move so quickly."

Jim stirs his rum and Coke with his index finger, his burger untouched.

"What a shitty day. No decent leads, nothing."

"People really didn't want to talk business and I don't blame them," Amber says, holding up a forkful of salad. "Time and place."

Tristan chimes in with a "don't worry about it." Was new business really the point?

"Of course it's the fucking point," says Jim.

"Jim just means…we expected more," says Maureen.

"I don't need a frickin' spokeswoman."

"Yeah right. Continue."

"This racket survives on relationships," says Jim.

He drains his glass.

"You two, the pair of you, might learn that some day."

The presentation of tournament prizes begins. Standing in front of a table of mini-trophies, a tanned AtlanticAssure VP talks about the company's community focus, client service orientation, and recent "strategic acquisitions."

"Screw that, I need another rum," says Jim. "Want anything, Amber?"

"Nothing, thanks."

"Hey boss, I'm good, nothing for me, either," Tristan says. "Maureen's fine, too."

Jim pushes through the crowd and onto the deck, nearly mowing down a tournament volunteer. The screen door bounces and reverberates.

"Not necessary, Tristan," says Maureen. "No need."

"Anyway," says Amber, getting back to her salad. "Great party."

WHEN MAUREEN DRIVES into their double garage, Jim flips the trunk open with his own keys before the Volvo stops moving. He usually takes impeccable care of his clubs, carefully wiping and storing them like fine china on a special rack in their mudroom. Tonight, he yanks the golf bag from the trunk and throws it across the doorway, so that the club heads sticking out of the bag smash against the ceramic tiles of the mudroom floor.

"Good job," says Maureen. "Awesome day."

He grabs a can of beer from the fridge and goes out to the back deck. Maureen rifles through the medicine cupboard for an antihistamine for the mosquito bites.

Reactine non-drowsy. Nope.

Extra-strength Benadryl. The package says *May Cause Sedation*. Absolutely yes.

She washes down the pill with a mouthful of water and follows Jim outside, where he's planted on one of the striped chairs. Head in hands, fingertips on forehead.

"Shit, shit, shit," he repeats like a mantra. Then he starts to cry, head down and shoulders shaking. Tears fall on the table's glass surface.

Maureen sits.

"Again," she says. "This?"

The couple hold their positions as the daylight wanes. The temperature has finally dropped and a new breeze keeps the bugs at bay. In perfect timing with the fading sun, the cul-de-sac's Saturday lawnmower racket subsides. Then, in the fresh silence, a different sound from next door—footsteps and the squeak of a sliding door. The lots are long and narrow in their neighbourhood, so noises tend to drift.

"What good does this do?" Maureen whispers. "Any of it."

Next door, their neighbour Richie calls to his wife, Marina:

"Coming? Drinks are ready. Jesus, I think just I saw a bat."

"A rat? No!"

"I said bat. Don't be paranoid."

At the sound of the neighbour's voice, Maureen rises and flips on the deck light.

"If you're going to stay out," she says softly, hoping Jim will match her volume.

The light is harsh; it triggers an off-switch for Jim's tears. He blinks and wipes his eyes. Light jazz trickles over from twenty feet away.

"I embarrassed you. No. I embarrassed us," he says quietly.

"We did our best," she says. "There's no shame in any of it."

Jim massages his forehead with grimy hands.

"Bargain-hunting vulture pricks."

His wife turns into the house, closes the door gently behind her. She passes the unsigned documents on their countertop that will hand Sullivan Insurance over to AtlanticAssure. Jim and Maureen will be gone in three months; the contract stipulates that Amber and Tristan will be in charge. They understand the digital potential of the business inside and out, have fresh ideas. It makes sense.

Maureen had been the one to run the numbers. She calculated the deal could, finally, pay off the line of credit, but would not be enough to save the house.

They'd sell. Neighbours would assume they'd made a killing when they snooped online, but the Sullivans' equity was minimal. They'd search for a reasonably priced apartment in the outskirts. Hand back the keys to Jim's leased Volvo and hope Maureen's 2017 Corolla would hold up.

Tell their daughter, tell everyone they know a semi-retirement lie, then look for new jobs.

Maureen pours amaretto into a wineglass, drinks it, and refills. She and her liqueur climb the stairs to their bedroom and move directly into the ensuite bathroom. She undresses and throws down her clothes, foul with pesticide, sweat, and sunscreen. Then cranks open the bathroom window and turns on the taps of the soaker tub only she uses.

The golf shirt is a pale yellow clump of synthetic on the floor. A glass base on the bathroom counter holds three candles. They're dusty. She'd lit them once and the wax had dripped down the sides too quickly, and after that she never remembered that she needed matches until she was already stripped bare. On the floor is a grey wool basket with a stack of books she plans to read some day.

The tub is twenty-two-inches deep and set into a tile platform. Getting in is like climbing over a low wall but she has a system: sit on the wide, faux marble rim and swing her legs over. She perches naked on the edge of the tub and reaches for her magnifying hand mirror.

It takes a half-dozen cotton pads and oily liquid to scrape the makeup off her face, before she can finally ease into the tub's warmth.

Everything aches.

She examines her body: Her breasts, one larger than the other, hang over a layer of fat that begins at the top of her ribs. Stiff, brown hairs emerging on random sites from belly to toes. The thickness of her waist and hips, further bloated from the humidity. The mosquito bites, red blotches on her calves and thighs and arms, dried blood now dissolved in the bath water. She grasps a few inches of tissue under her breast and then moves down the side of her body, waist to hip to bum. Runs her fingers along the faded caesarean scar, tucked below the roll that marks the end of her stomach and the beginning of her pubic hairline. A silent inventory.

Music drifts up from below. The Eagles. Jim must be in the basement, cleaning his golf clubs in the bathroom down there. Stereo cranked, he'll scrub the clubs one by one with a rough brush. With a bit of effort, he'll coax the marshmallow off his new driver. He'll then wipe his golf bag with a soft cloth and ease the clubs back in. All except the putter. He'll carry the putter to a narrow, ten-foot path of Astroturf laid out on the rec room floor, an indoor putting green with an automatic ball return.

She sips her drink, already drowsy from the Benadryl. She'll be groggy in the morning, but oblivion is worth it. Maybe tomorrow the inflammation will ease if she resists the temptation to scratch; the bites might heal quickly. Maureen downs the rest of the liqueur, shuts her eyes. She pictures Jim taking a ball from his pocket, laying it on the green, and thumping it straight into the putting chamber. He is good at this, rarely misses. The ball will pop out, roll down the little highway of artificial green, and come right back to him.

Pop, roll, return. Pop, roll, return.

She awakes to Jim tapping on the bathroom door. "Everything okay in there?"

"I'm coming," she says.

Climbing out of the tub is tough. She can't lift herself from a sitting position; that puts too much pressure on her wrists and what if she falls backward? No, the sensible way out is to flip over onto hands and knees and position her palms on the tub rim. Rise slowly and rest on the tiled edge before swinging her legs over to the floor.

The workaround works—she makes it out safely. Still, she remains on the edge, wet feet on the floor. Her elbows and breasts rest on damp thighs. The bath mat has slid out of reach so she drips directly onto the white tile. It is going to be slippery. She has forgotten her bathrobe, and the towel rack is bare.

"Maureen?" Jim asks again.

But on the other side, there is no rush to move. She reaches for her empty glass and raises it again. There's nothing left, but she still licks the edges, tasting the remains of amaretto, sickly sweet.

The Waiting Room

ONE OF THE FEW PEOPLE I SEE REGULARLY IS DR. TREMBLAY. PHD, not a physician. The non-doctor Dr. Tremblay instructs me to keep a diary. Journalling is supposedly the key. Write down the negative thoughts and counter them with rational, "realistic" statements. "Wax poetic" about the burnout, the meltdown, the relationship implosion, the DUI (charges dropped on a technicality). Write about extended sick leave. About the need to extend extended sick leave as far as it can possibly extend.

Standard cognitive behavioural therapy, or is it dialectical? Blah blah blah hippy crap. No thanks—I'm enjoying the time off, full stop.

Today Dr. Tremblay informs me, real-doctor, Dr. Rebecca Findlay, that I have made impressive progress. That I have a "robust tool box" for my condition. Perhaps it's time to ease back into work.

"Can't be done," I say.

"Can't be done?"

"I need my routine, need my swim."

With an unsubtle eyebrow raise, Dr. Tremblay suggests I alter the routine. Take a lunch break, go outside, fit in a swim in the evenings.

"You're a good surgeon," she says. "They need you. The system. We need you doing your job. People need you."

People.

At the end I didn't see them as people. I saw them as fifteen or twenty feet of pulsing, coiled duodenum, ileum, jejunum, colon, and rectum. I saw them through a helmet-mounted camera, through an incision, bellies pumped up and bloated with carbon dioxide. As sigmoidectomies, ileostomies, and sphincterotomies. Crohn's in the morning, a couple of cancers in the afternoon. Diverticulitis and anal fissures on a Friday night.

"What they require is perfection," I reply. "And that's not me."

I don't have the energy to explain that her brilliant strategy—take lunch breaks for quiet walks and salads, gently drift out of the hospital at will to go for a swim—is ludicrous. No one wants that type of colleague. No one will welcome a part-timer who doesn't do their share on a production line with an infinite conveyor belt of bodies.

Either you're all in, or you're out. And I am out.

Dr. Tremblay is too subtle to baldly ask me how this or that "makes me feel" but instead enquires, "If everyone in your life saw you for who you really are, what would that look like?"

After a careful pause to signify I'm giving the query serious thought, I answer: "I need to reflect on that. I feel that I'm just at the beginning of this journey."

I've become proficient at therapy speak. The strategy is to dole out just enough to keep her from telling the insurance company that I'm ready for the operating room.

"Who are you if you're not going to work every day?" asks Dr. Tremblay.

That's an easy one.

"A person with a life."

FOR SOME PEOPLE, swimming laps in a twenty-five-metre pool is an exercise in futility. Back and forth, back and forth. Tedious, mind-numbing activity leading nowhere. In the past, that's how I would have viewed it.

Now I know better. I'm a serious swimmer and I know what serious swimmers know. We understand the thought-dissolving peace to be found in graceful repetition. We ignore the sting of the chlorine, the damp grimy floors of the change rooms, the initial cold shock as we immerse our bodies. We concentrate: Tilt our heads above the water to breathe in, tilt back to breathe out, all while propelling ourselves across the length of a concrete rectangle. Go, don't push. That's essential: You go, but you never push. Eyes straight ahead and wide open inside tight goggles. Mind empty, body focused on the glide and the rhythm. Twenty-five metres, a flip turn—an underwater somersault, weightless gymnastics—and another twenty-five.

When we share lanes, we divide ourselves according to ability so that we move at the same speed and form an endless circle.

The morning swim is the core of my routine. I start the day with a mug of lemon-water, a bowl of oatmeal with flax seed and a teaspoon of brown sugar. Then off to the pool, bathing suit underneath my clothes. My high-tech Speedo is so tight it's difficult to unroll over my stomach and boobs, but it feels good. The material makes me more buoyant. The straps criss-cross my back, freeing my shoulders. The fabric compresses my muscles. I bought three of these suits online after extensive research; they reduce drag, the invisible force that slows us down.

After an hour of steady lengths, I shower and change. At first I would change in a toilet stall, banging my soaked ass and arms against the Formica walls. Over the past eight months, smoothly defined muscle has emerged. Recently I joined the rest of the naked bodies in the locker room, thanks to two plush new towels with a band of Velcro at the top. I alternate between a fuchsia and a deep turquoise towel. With the terry cloth securing my torso, I can unpeel my swimsuit and put on bra and underpants before shedding the damp cloth and rolling it into a neat cylinder to fit into my kit bag.

I started off swimming during the midmorning session, but the pool was littered with seniors and oddballs. One day, an older lady had a meltdown in the pool, screaming about garbage in the water and cursing the lifeguards, and throwing all the pool noodles around. Straight up berserko stuff.

This was not the vibe I needed for this part of my process, so I switched over to early mornings. I figured that's where I'd find the athletes, and I was correct.

These are my people.

On Saturdays, a small group goes for coffee after the swim. One of the women, a lawyer named Elizabeth, invited me along a few weeks ago and I accepted. Now I can honestly tell Dr. Tremblay that I'm trying to make friends to replace the phonies who vaporized when I left the hospital.

The swimmer/lawyer asked what "I do" and when I said I'm on a medical leave, she didn't ask any more questions.

I'd expected coffee conversation to focus on time trials, stroke improvement, maybe how to avoid a damaged rotator cuff. But they talk about their gardens, what's good at the farmers' market, the rain/snow/heat we've been subjected to, what they're watching on their devices these days.

There's a pattern to it, and I am learning how to say the right things to seem like I'm part of it too, encouraging this genre of casual, impersonal chit-chat.

IN THE AFTERNOONS my routine demands a one-hour walk at the Frog Pond, a park with a web of trails along the Northwest Arm, a few blocks from my new condo. The only person in the building I know or speak to, aside from a nod in the hallway or elevator, is Mrs. Vucovic, the widow next door who must be in her late eighties.

She has an overly friendly beagle named Katya. On my afternoon walk one day, I meet Mrs. Vucovic and Katya on the park trail and they join me, uninvited, on a one-kilometre loop around the pond that, given its name, presumably is, or was, frog habitat. I have never seen a single frog there. This loop is usually just my starting point; on its own it isn't challenging, even twice around.

Mrs. Vucovic wears a fleece track suit, a floral hat, and carries a burgundy leather pouch that bulges with who knows what.

"You walk in the afternoons now," she says.

I'm startled. I have no clue how she knows this but I say, "Yes, I prefer an afternoon walk, Mrs. Vucovic."

"Vucovic," she says, replacing the hard c at the end with something like an "itch."

"But I am Vera," she says. "You call me Vera."

"Vera," I say. "Okay. I'm Rebecca."

"You do not go to the hospital anymore, Rebecca," she continues.

"Not right now."

This would be the time to speed up, leave the old lady and her dog behind, but my rhythm slows, and my stride shortens to match their pace.

Mrs. Vucovic—Vera—persists.

"You do not go to work anymore. But you do not seem sick."

She stops walking and eyes me head to toe.

"You rest?"

I nod. I don't know why I am putting up with this.

"Katya needs more rest too, now," she says, comparing me to her dog, who is now illegally off leash and dawdling behind us.

"You go ahead," says Vera, gesturing with a bright pink cane. But I stick around.

For the rest of our glacially paced walk, Vera inventories each of her grandchildren: names, ages, current state of finding their way in the world. It's oddly mesmerizing. I interject a few polite words, and she keeps talking.

"One of my granddaughters asked us to call her they, and now she, they, has a girlfriend."

"Is that okay?"

"Sure, why not? They had to go to Alberta for good jobs. Engineers, both. They make good salaries and take very nice trips. They set me up on the WhatsApp to send pictures."

After this, Vera appears at my door a few days a week with food. One day, a soup; another day, stew with warm biscuits.

"You need to eat," she says, looking over my shoulder at the unpacked boxes on the floor, the naked windows, and the lack of furniture.

I lift the lids expecting to find exotic dishes with beets and turnips, meals with unpronounceable Eastern European names, but find chicken soup thickened with too many noodles, casseroles, roast pork.

One day I say, "I wouldn't mind trying one of the soups from your country sometime."

Vera laughs.

"I learned to make food from the *Better Homes and Gardens* cookbook, in Canada. If you can read a book, Rebecca, you can cook."

I RUN INTO Dr. Tremblay at the grocery store. She's wearing workout clothes but still looks clean, crisp, and intact. Even her white-and-pink running shoes are pristine, as if they never touch the ground. She walks past me in the produce section and even when I say hello, my own psychologist doesn't recognize me, or maybe pretends not to for professional reasons, like "our kind of talking is not this kind of talking."

But I say hello again and either something clicks and she knows who I am, or she realizes she can't avoid me. We chat about the wonderful autumn weather; how great it is that even the big grocery chains offer local fruit and vegetables nowadays. I'd like to believe that if you overheard us, you would assume we were neighbours or colleagues. I absolutely feel that I held up my end of the conversation.

While we talk, I analyze her groceries. Lots of leafy greens. Fruit, quinoa, and fresh salmon. Nothing in a box.

It occurs to me that my own cart looks a lot like Dr. Tremblay's. That could be a problem; I worry that I have the grocery cart of an efficient, capable professional, not the cart of a burnout who should be banned from the OR indefinitely. It might be more convincing if the cart were stuffed with nachos, pop, frozen pizza, the crap that people who have out-of-control lives call groceries.

There's a long line at the checkout. I look to the right and left, ahead and behind, curious about what everyone else is buying. I discover mine is the only cart containing nothing from the treat category. It is devoid of even a sodium-reduced cracker. But apparently there are households where boneless, skinless chicken breasts can peacefully coexist with Double Stuf Oreos, where they snack on Pizza Pockets as well as celery. Healthy-looking people nonchalantly stack romaine lettuce, red peppers, and hothouse tomatoes on the counter alongside snacks packaged in unnatural but seductively cheery colours. Cheezies and Sour Patch Kids.

I have the urge to back up my cart to explore the aisles I never visit, but I can't reverse without disrupting the flow of the queue. Then I notice Dr. Tremblay join a line a few rows over.

A family-size, sunshine-yellow bag of No Name barbecue chips peeks out through the metal bars of her cart.

AT OUR NEXT session, Dr. Tremblay says we need to get serious about the back-to-work plan.

"I can't. I just can't," I say.

This is a problem. I always knew, at some point, she would be obliged to sign an insurance form indicating that I'm fit to work. If she doesn't, the insurance company will eventually hire their own medical professional to scrutinize me. They could even order a full-on psychiatric assessment because this disability claim, like me, is expensive.

Back to the OR. That is the last thing I want. That, I know for sure. The problem is, I don't know the first thing I want. Or the second thing, or anything.

Dr. Tremblay takes off her glasses and lets them hang from an elegant chain around her neck, leans forward, and lays her chin on folded hands.

"Is there anything we haven't talked about yet that we need to address?"

We could finally talk about failure, I could say, but do not. Being single again is failure. Never having children and now it's too late. Failure.

No furniture in your new condo. No drapes in your new living room. Scruffy, unmatched towels. Shame on you.

Burnout equals failure. Leaving medicine, or even taking a break, slowing down, is failure. Staying, but being less than perfect, less than, is failure. Screw up a procedure and you get sued for malpractice. Screw up the paperwork and hospital administration is all over you. Be anything less than a fictional TV doctor holding everyone's hand, spending precious time you don't have explaining every tiny, irrelevant detail. They complain to the medical society and you get a note on your file about your communications skills and they force you to waste a week at some workshop. Never mind I cut out your festering cancer and saved your life.

I look at Dr. Tremblay. She reeks of non-failure: serene, fit, dressed in a cashmere sweater and black pants that are so simple they must be expensive; a gorgeous, chocolate-brown tote bag tucked next to her desk. Discreet makeup and minimalist gold jewellery.

"Nope," I say. "Nothing else."

"Because if you aren't able to be honest with me, maybe you're better off seeing someone else," she says and leans back on her leather chair.

I say nothing. Just shrug.

"We won't decide today. We meet again next week," she says. "We'll discuss it then."

I need to change the tone of this appointment, to redirect to safer ground, so I reveal that every Sunday I phone my parents in Toronto to tell them about my pretend hospital shifts that week. This is true.

"And how does that work?" she asks, instantly engaged.

"It's easier than you'd think. I come from doctors. They hear what they want to hear. My mother can look at a cerebral cortex and understand it, and my father can examine an aorta and see things few other people can. But when it comes to their own daughter's thoughts and feelings, these 'specialists' of the mind and the heart are totally clueless."

This is material no psychologist could resist excavating. By introducing this line of discussion, I hope to buy some time.

ONE MORNING, I'M about to leave for the pool when there's a knock at the door. It's Vera in her mauve dog-walking outfit, her favourite.

"I need you," she says. "You must help."

I follow her next door. Katya is lying across her pink, faux fur doggie bed, as if asleep. Vera strokes the dog's ears, tells me that Katya practically crawled to her bed last night. It seemed like she had stiff legs. But things took a turn and Vera woke up at 3:00 A.M. to the dog's laboured breathing. Then the sound stopped, or maybe Katya just began to breathe very lightly.

"Maybe she is in a coma?" she asks.

I bend down and run my palm over her velvety head. I flip her over and run my hands along the length of her body. I search for a pulse, even a weak one.

Oh, Katya.

She's still warm but there is no life in her liquid chocolate eyes. We sit on the floor. We linger, Vera and I linger, unwilling to lift our hands from Katya.

Eventually, Vera says, "I cannot lift her, I cannot carry her alone."

"I know," I say, even though Katya only weighs about twenty pounds. "May I carry her for you?"

"Yes, please, Rebecca."

I help Vera get up from the floor. We decide it's best to leave Katya on her comfy bed. I reach under the pink fluff on the long ends, making a cradle that I lift with care.

"We'll take my car," I say. "We'll go wherever we need to go."

We walk together down the long condo hallway and enter the elevator. We ride down to the parking garage, where I slide the Katya bundle onto the back seat of my Accord.

"I will stay with her," says Vera, getting into the back seat.

"Of course."

I check the vet clinic location on my phone, assess the options, and proceed on a route that minimizes delay. The morning traffic is building but we're going against the flow, heading to a suburban strip mall. I hear Vera whispering. Her words aren't clear but the tone is soothing and soft. Comforting. From what I can make out, it seems she is thanking Katya.

Despite Google Maps, we get stuck in a traffic muddle, trapped behind a city roadwork crew with a rotating Stop/Go sign. The Stop sign lasts an eternity as we watch a stream of cars speed by in the other direction.

"I'm sorry about this holdup," I say to Vera's reflection in the rear-view mirror.

"Rebecca, there is no rush for Katya, no rush for me."

When we finally make it to the vet clinic, we lift the dog together and carry her in. There's an old man with a sleeping poodle in his lap in the otherwise empty waiting room. A receptionist in her twenties sits behind a glass screen, staring at a computer.

"One moment," she says.

We wait. I sniff loudly as if I have allergies or a cold. This person, wearing medical scrubs, I notice, and a dozen or so gaudy rings on her fingers, says, "Just a minute," and continues to stare at her computer.

I wait a reasonable amount of time, maybe thirty or forty more seconds.

"Excuse me," I say. "We would appreciate some assistance."

"Katya, my dog. She is gone," Vera adds. "My dog has died."

I look over at her, holding up the other side, her end of the dog bed, and I imagine how heavy it must be, the strain on those octogenarian arm muscles. We are both stuck in the same position with Katya resting between us.

The young woman in the bogus medical scrubs drags her eyes away from the screen. She takes in the old lady, the dog, me.

"I'm very sorry for your loss," she says without warmth.

They must give them a list of things to say because she doesn't look like she means it. Siri would display more empathy.

"Thank you," says Vera, accepting the insincere condolence with grace.

"I'm afraid you'll have to go back outside, though, and take it around to the back door."

The receptionist points to the exit with a ringed finger.

"Deceased animals aren't permitted in the reception area."

"That's no way to speak to a person," I say in what I hope is an intimidating tone.

But the receptionist is not flustered. She has been through this before, probably hundreds of times.

"If you had called first, I would have instructed you," she says.

I try to meet her eye again, but she's back to her screen.

We carry Katya around the building to the back door. We lower the dog to the ground, I ring a doorbell, and we wait. It takes a few minutes and a few more doorbell rings but finally a vet tech and the duty vet take over, lifting Katya onto a cart. They roll the cart into what looks like an operating room, but with the lights dimmed. They lay her body on a metal table.

The tech leaves for a few minutes to pull Katya's file, while the vet asks Vera if she'd like to spend a few more minutes with her.

"No," she says, unbuckling Katya's floral collar with arthritic fingers. "We are fine now."

Vera doesn't hesitate with the few decisions left: Cremation? Yes. Keep the ashes? No.

Since she will not return to collect ashes, Vera must pay a disposal bill today. She forgot her purse, only has her house key, so I pull out my Amex.

"WE WERE IN and out of there in about forty-five minutes," I tell Dr. Tremblay the next day.

"What happened next?"

"Vera was quiet on the drive home. At the apartment, she handed me her keys and I unlocked her door. She sent me away, said she needed a nap. I went back to my place. Then I noticed I was still wearing my dry bathing suit underneath my clothes. The shoulder straps were digging into my skin."

Dr. Tremblay jots a note on her lined pad without looking down. I appreciate that she still uses paper.

"I knocked on her door in the afternoon to check on her, and Vera's daughter answered. We'd met before, in passing. There was a granddaughter there too. They'd brought food— muffins and cookies and fruit. They invited me in, were polite enough, but I didn't want to intrude."

"And..."

"I went back to my own apartment, put on a jacket, and went for my afternoon walk."

"Back to the usual routine."

"Yeah."

VERA GOES UNDER the radar for a few weeks, and I don't pursue her. But then a knock at the door one day after lunch.

"Rebecca, we can walk together today?"

I'm tempted to say I'm not available. Without Katya, who knows where this might lead? But I nod yes.

"Very good. First, we will have coffee. Come."

I follow her into the too warm apartment and slide onto my usual chair at her tiny kitchen table. I watch her scoop and measure the coffee, top up the water in the coffee maker. She presses the brew button and we are quiet as the machine does its work. She peels plastic wrap off a plate of sliced banana bread, pours me a black coffee.

There's a window in her kitchen. I notice her apartment gets the afternoon sun, realize that means my own place must get the afternoon sun too.

"The children say get another dog, but I won't decide now."

"Of course," I say.

Vera sips her coffee. "Rebecca, I have a story for you. I remembered this in the past few days."

She tells me that in post-war Rijeka, Croatia, when she was a little girl, there was an old man who climbed down a metal ladder to the Adriatic to swim every day. Her aunts said he had been a soldier in the first war but when he came home, he was not the same. He refused to leave his bed, barely ate. Only spoke a few words. They sent for the doctor, who coaxed him down to the sea, into the water.

"Where people swam, it was just a bare concrete platform with a ladder, not fancy," says Vera.

The doctor and his patient swam together every day. Soon the patient could swim alone.

"This is his medicine. He swims in the sea every day for the rest of his life. Some days the water is warm and calm, and on others the waves are cold and harsh. But he jumps in every day, this man," says Vera.

I see what she's attempting with this story.

"So this is about how important doctors are, how they make a difference."

"No."

"Are you saying I should go back to the hospital, back to work? Just try it?"

"No, Rebecca."

"No?"

"Rebecca, I was just thinking, being so sad about Katya, that it would be maybe good for me to go the pool like you do. My daughter says they have seniors' aquafit on Mondays and Wednesdays."

"Oh."

"Of course, what you say may also be true," she says, spreading unnecessary butter on her banana bread.

AT MY NEXT therapy appointment, Dr. Tremblay probes me about the drinking and driving charge. I repeat that the DUI was a nothing sandwich, an aberration. I was barely over the line and they dropped it when the cop messed up the paperwork.

I change the topic. "I want to tell you about my last day at work."

"Absolutely," she says, turning a page in her notebook. We've never discussed this.

The patient chair in her office is a padded swivel model, high end, so I swivel. It helps to move as I talk, even just back and forth.

"I did my morning rounds, met with a case in his mid-seventies who was being discharged. Colon cancer, stage two, routine procedure. Then his wife bombarded me with questions about how to take care of him at home. I told her a nurse would give them a pamphlet on their way out. The patient didn't say much but kept looking at me like he expected—or wanted—something more. They always want more.

"You're alive, I thought. Shouldn't that be enough?"

Dr. Tremblay holds her pen between her white, even teeth and looks over her glasses at me. "I think we both know there's something more than just being alive. Right?"

"Right. Anyway. I went to the hospital cafeteria for coffee and a sandwich. They'd scheduled me for surgeries all afternoon and into the evening. Then I'd have the paperwork to catch up on. I was behind. I'm always behind.

"I checked my phone. There was a text from my ex, bugging me about when I could pick up the rest of my things. Nothing hostile, she was only looking for information. There was a bill from the lawyer who'd handled the DUI charge. An email from the medical society about some seminar on empathetic patient communication."

Dr. Tremblay surprises me with a smile. "Maybe vet clinics should have those seminars too."

"Yup."

"I'm sorry, Rebecca. I interrupted. Please go on."

"It's okay." I pick up the glass of water that she always gives me but I rarely touch. I swallow a mouthful and put it down.

"The cafeteria was packed, jammed, so I waited in line with everyone else. Then I suddenly felt something bad happening. Something terrible. Like I was in danger.

"I was sweating, clammy. The room closed in like a tunnel. I couldn't breathe, I was vibrating. Chest pains. I slid to the floor and checked my Fitbit. My heart rate was 145, 175, 190. Then they surrounded me, these doctors and nurses on their coffee breaks. These ordinary people visiting sick people. These scared sick people finally in for tests after months of waiting. All this attention for some random physician sprawled on the floor."

Dr. Tremblay signals with a slight eye widening and an encouraging almost-smile. She knows, of course, that there's more.

"Within minutes I was on a gurney," I continue. "They rolled me downstairs. They rushed me through the ER waiting room. It was crowded, people standing, a few lying on the floor. Lots of coughing. We raced by all those people waiting their turn. People of all colours, all ages, every one of them saw me speed by in my white coat. All in one whoosh.

"We rolled past security into the ER. Didn't stop at the reception desk. They manoeuvred me through a hallway obstructed with gurneys. Whoosh, we bypassed them, too."

Dr. Tremblay taps her lips with the pen. "With your white coat on."

"Yes."

I look around her office for a moment, at her university degrees on the wall, at her framed licence. I could stop talking now but decide it's time to continue.

"Right away, like immediately, stat, pronto, they wheeled me into a private room in the ER. They gave me an ECG, took blood samples, monitored my blood pressure. Nurses were in and out. A cardiologist checked me, said she would see me in her office next week, that she had already scheduled a stress test. She gave me a heart monitor to wear at home for a few days. Just a precaution, she said, but 'we have to take care of each other, Dr. Findlay.'"

I stop, needing to catch my breath again. Dr. Tremblay waits. I don't feel pressured or rushed.

"Any regular person—any non-physician person—wouldn't even have made it into the ER hallway at this point," I explain, as if I need to.

"They should have made me wait, Dr. Tremblay. They should have made me wait like everyone else."

She writes a little bit and looks back up at me. Not staring, just looking.

"You felt that way then? Or do you feel that way now?" she asks.

The digital clock on her desk alerts me that there are four minutes left in today's session. Her next appointment is probably already in the reception area, waiting because they have no choice, hoping for a solution she can't possibly deliver in a fifty-five-minute slot. And I am so tired. But the good kind, like after sixty laps of the pool.

"Look, I only know now," I say. "Today that's all I have for you."

"Fair enough, Dr. Findlay," my doctor replies.

Then we both stand up at the same time. She puts her pad and pen down on the side table and we turn toward the door. As I move away, I look over and briefly catch a glimpse at the top, last, most recent page. These are her notes, written in a cryptic, looping scrawl I can't decipher or decode.

Plan for a Snowblower

MIDDLE-AGED, LONG-TERM RELATIONSHIP SEX. IT CAN BE efficient without being mechanical. This Sunday afternoon in December, the threat of interruption by returning teenagers ratchets up Dave and Christine's pace. Time is precious. Every urgent move has a purpose: his hand, here, her mouth, right there.

Christine and Dave switch places. Her turn on top. She moves the way she needs to move; his job is to maintain the whole situation. His fingers go down, grazing stretch marks that are invisible to his eye, that feel, to him, like soft, smooth, warm skin. Further over, he finds the place where the curve of her butt greets the back of her thigh. There, his touch meets a strange resistance, a patch of subtle roughness, a spot she wouldn't be able to see without yogic contortion.

He stops what he's doing. Runs his hand over the spot again, inspection disguised as caress. This is unexpected. Skin that hasn't seen the sun since she ran naked on the beach as a toddler. The part of her that skims the border of public and private.

Christine notices the change. How the hell could she not notice?

She stops too. Rolls off.

"Everything all right?"

"Sorry," he says.

"Don't apologize," she murmurs, inching closer. They're side by side now, bare stomach to bare stomach. She presses her sixty-one-inch frame into his long body, and he curls to form a crescent around her.

"It's ok if you want to take a break."

He does not want to alarm her, fears upsetting her, but needs to investigate. He slides his hand down her back, finds the rough, scaly patch again.

"I feel something," he says. "There's something new down here that we should check."

Christine doesn't hesitate. She lifts her left arm, gently nudges his fingers away to feel for herself.

"Oh," she says. She doesn't flinch, never has.

Whenever he rails on about unfairness, asks why the fuck does cancer keep coming after her, she shrugs.

Whenever he asks why, when she's diligent about zinc frigging SPF 50, doesn't smoke, doesn't drink, marches through ten thousand steps a day—why does it keep coming—she lets him rant but does not participate.

"Turn on the lights," she says, as focused now as a person can be.

Dusk has passed; their bedroom is dark except for the invasive streetlight that creeps in uninvited along the edges of their curtains. Custom curtains—flowery, not Dave and Christine's taste but too thick and expensive to throw out—left by the home's previous owners. He switches on his bedside lamp and she switches on hers. The lamps don't match but they suit. The bulbs are too bright, though; he bought the wrong replacements and meant to replace the replacements, but time got away. Maybe his mistake was on purpose, he wonders now. In this situation, their bedroom cannot be too bright.

Dave says, "I'll get the magnifying glass," and his wife lies on her stomach and spreads her legs, preparing for scrutiny.

SINCE HER FIRST melanoma, Dave has been delegated the areas of his wife's body that are inaccessible to her. She has deputized him to check the back of her hairline, to be accountable for the skin on her upper, middle, and lower back. Her buttocks. For scanning it all. He appraises all her new, misshapen, and irregularly pigmented bits. Then reports his findings.

He prefers to work in natural light. They open the back drapes in their bedroom to bring in the sun and the evergreens in the yard shield them. On the morning of the first day of each month, she strips, stands still and nude. She positions herself off to the side of the window just in case a neighbour can peek through the trees. He hands her a coffee and examines the back of her body with an illuminated magnifying glass they found at the drugstore. He rubs the moles she has had since her teens. Has the texture changed? The colour, the size, the shape? When he comes upon something he doesn't like the look or feel of, he takes a picture in extreme close-up to show her.

Christine then sits on their comforter and inspects herself—the parts she can see—and only occasionally asks for a second opinion. She is thorough, checking between her toes, under fingernails, lifting each breast, patiently searching for evidence of epidermal betrayal.

The dermatologist has taught them what to look for, but warned that sometimes melanoma doesn't look like what we think it might. View any change in a mole or a freckle, or any new growth, with suspicion.

"Come to me with anything that concerns you," she'd said. That was three years—six malignancies—ago. Right shoulder, left shoulder, lower neck, lower back, lower back again, inner right calf. All but the calf detected by Dave, patches that hadn't been painful or scabby or even itchy but malignant nonetheless. Some of the surgeries have left bumpy scars. The skin on a person's back is already tight; the surgeon had warned his work would be effective but not pretty, and it wasn't.

The right shoulder excision had been especially problematic. Infected stitches. Dave had noticed first. A few days after the surgery, he spied a worrisome leak from under the dressing. Christine was adamant; the nurses said don't remove the dressing for three days. But Dave insisted harder than she resisted and convinced her to allow him to peel off the bandage. Despite the surgeon's warning, he was shocked at how messy and irregular the stitches were—Christine's sock darning efforts were neater—but did not comment on the workmanship. Was alarmed but not surprised to see the uneven stitches were yellow with pus. He took a photo and enlarged it, his finger circling the obvious infection, to convince her to call the clinic.

They filled the antibiotic prescription on the way home and he bought a bottle of water so she could take her first pill in the car.

He is always careful with her body. Has been since she matter-of-factly informed him on their third date about what had happened when she was a teenager.

ON TUESDAY AFTERNOON, Dave stands at their front bedroom window watching snow converge on their short, steep driveway. In a few minutes the pavement will disappear. The forecast is for twenty centimetres. It wasn't supposed to start for several hours.

"But here we are," he says.

Christine is cleaning out her side of the closet. There's a "stay" pile, a "go" pile, and a "maybe" pile.

A walk-in closet is typical for this type of house but it far exceeds any she has ever owned or rented or shared. Between Dave and Christine's belongings, it isn't even half full, but she reorganizes her closet every winter and summer, no matter what its size. Even if she doesn't end up with a big donation pile, there's always a loose button to sew, a pilled sweater to comb, or shoes with rundown heels to deal with.

Dave watches her appraise a vintage wool cardigan with pearl buttons, a treasure scored at a charity thrift store. There's no way she'll let that go, he thinks, just before it is carefully folded and placed in the "stay" pile.

There's a bandage under Christine's pants but it doesn't prevent her from sitting on the hardwood floor. Her dermatologist's receptionist had called Monday afternoon after hearing her Sunday voicemail. She offered an 8:15 appointment for this morning. Christine is on their list of people they'll work in before official office hours. Today, her dermatologist froze her skin, cut out a slice, and sent it for a quickie biopsy. The doctor's thirty-seven years of experience says "malignant," so she has already sent a referral to the same surgeon who sliced out the depths and margins of all previous rogue moles and growths.

"Let's not wait until we have a firm answer," she said. "I don't like the look of it."

After the appointment, Dave decided to take the day off. His government IT job allows many types of leave. Christine's job doesn't, but she wasn't scheduled to work at the nursing home today anyway.

The snowfall is picking up. He has worked this driveway for two winters now and it is not good. There are stone retaining walls on either side that act almost like a fortress moat, and if there is in any moisture at all in the snow, and it gets heavy, it is almost impossible to lift those thousands of shovelfuls over the top.

"We really should buy a snowblower," Dave says, laying his palm on the cold window, leaving a handprint on the condensation.

These casement windows look fancy but are poor quality. Dave figures the previous owners chose them for style, not substance. Cold wind penetrates the substandard glass. He runs a finger along the bottom edge, where a thin layer of ice is growing. In this house they can barely afford, stretched themselves to purchase, the windows annoy him. In winter, they contend with ice; in summer, they battle mildew.

"A snowblower to share. We can't justify getting our own, I don't think," he says.

In his last neighbourhood, where he'd lived as a divorced dad before marrying Christine, four families pooled their money and bought a midrange Toro.

"How do you think that would work with this crowd?" she asks.

She has just put on a sleeveless blouse and stands with her back to the dresser mirror. Then she holds up her purse compact to see how the shirt looks from behind.

Dave silently predicts it will go in the "maybe" pile, and after she peels it off, it does.

He explains how his snowblower co-op would work: Three or four, ideally four, neighbours each chip in $300. Dave could organize snow days. If someone needs to get out of their driveway early, they use the snowblower first. People with flexible schedules or who work from home would be next. If someone can't handle the machine, Dave would blow out their driveway for them.

"If these people want a snowblower, they already own one," says Christine. "If you appear at their door, they'll assume 'that guy wants to borrow my snowblower.'"

They weren't exactly welcomed with open arms when they moved in. Nobody popped by to deliver welcome-to-the-neighbourhood cookies. No one even said hello. But no one was hostile either, Dave pointed out. The people on this street just kept to themselves. They all had attached garages, which meant they came and went like ghosts. Instead of front porches, the houses all had back decks with wooden privacy screens. Christine and Dave had a deck themselves, three levels, so who were they to judge? He knew the neighbours better than Christine, would chat with the older man named Phil across the street when they were both raking leaves, would wave to the couple next door while he was weeding, said hello to the dog walkers, to the young parents pushing strollers and looking at their phones who didn't notice his greeting, to the walking-pole regulars who seemed to be on a perpetual mission.

"It's just an idea," says Dave.

Christine throws a stretched-out bathing suit onto the "go" pile.

"There's nothing wrong with the idea," she says. "It's a great idea in a certain type of world."

So far, the "go" pile includes worn-out panties, a few stained T-shirts, and a pair of pointy high heels that she bought on sale and regretted when they blistered her baby toes.

"Look, just don't be surprised if you go door-to-door like

an alarm system salesman, and they look at you like you're nuts," she says.

Dave is drifting back to the dermatologist's response when he'd asked if it was a bad sign, that the growth was in a spot that was not, had not, been exposed to the sun.

"We can't be sure," she said, taping the small dressing. "The important thing is you're here now and we're addressing it."

Christine is throwing the contents of her sock drawer onto the bed, tidy rolled ball by tidy rolled ball.

"Realistically, though," she asks. "Who do you think will be interested?"

A FEW DAYS LATER, they hang out in their bedroom after supper. Their kids—his daughter, her youngest son—have friends over. One group has claimed the rec room and the other occupies the kitchen. Christine has just settled in on her side of the bed with the latest *Thursday Night Murder Club*. She waited for months and her turn has arrived. After languishing at number seven on the library waiting list, she somehow popped to the top.

"I wish there were dozens of these," she says, examining the inside flap and back cover. She appreciates a distraction, but it isn't easy to track down a book or a show that's distracting in the right way. Dave's reading and watching taste trends to the post-apocalyptic, and that's not for her. On his side of the bed, he pretends to read a Stephen King novella on the iPad, but sneaks a look at mortgage renewal rates. "No money talk in the bedroom" is their rule but he has discovered, maybe created, a loophole: it's acceptable to scare the shit out of yourself about your shaky finances while sitting on the marital bed, just do not immediately share it with your partner.

They have a mortgage rate of 2.21 per cent. Oops, that expires soon, the bank had just reminded him again with a chirpy promotional email. If they don't decide on a new term, the bank will decide for them, will automatically assign an open term at the highest rate. As their limited options blink at Dave on the eight-inch screen, he interrogates himself. How could they have been so delusional to believe that interest rates would remain ridiculously low, that banks' money would indefinitely cost almost nothing, would be almost free?

Nothing lasts forever; they are both old enough to know that.

Mortgage rates are climbing. He needs to know the precise implications, what it will cost them, and punches numbers into an online calculator: mortgage amount, payment frequency, interest rate, and amortization. Catches his breath at the result. An extra $1,300 a month. He clicks the X to close the site, hopes Christine hasn't noticed what he's up to.

Money is already tight. Kids, mortgage, utilities, car loan, groceries.

At the beginning of the pandemic, real estate prices dipped briefly in Halifax, creating an opportunity, maybe their only chance, to buy a home together. The bank based the loan on their two salaries, a crazy-low, "introductory" interest rate, and a minimum down payment. They looked online and saw this house. It was big and in a good neighbourhood just off the Halifax peninsula. They lowballed an offer, and the sellers, an older couple retiring from the insurance business, accepted on the condition Dave and Christine agree to a quick closing date.

Christine had always hoped for a single-family home with an upstairs. Her life had been duplexes, apartments, bottom floors of rentals. She'd never had an ensuite bathroom, let alone one with a soaker tub. Soon, all of this will cost them more than $4,200 every month.

Dave knows they need to figure out what to do, but this is not the time. He has no clue when the right time will be, what conditions must be present, but now is not the time.

Christine's phone rings. She gestures for a pen and paper, and then jots down a note before saying thank you and hanging up.

"Shit. It's another one," she says. "Surgery next Friday."

"Sooner would be better," he says and instantly regrets his words. To make up for it, he adds, "Good that they'll call after hours."

"Nothing to do but wait," she says, picking up her book. He notices it takes her an unusually long time to read two pages and flip to the next.

DAVE WALKS AWAY from the house. He heads down the hill to make his initial pitch for the snowblower cooperative. He set out as soon as he got home from work, hoping he wouldn't irritate people by interrupting their supper.

Christine's ass excavation, as they're calling it, went well. They think. They don't know yet if it really went well, but the excision is healing nicely with no infection. They're waiting for a pathology report that their surgeon will explain. Christine will ask multiple follow-up questions until she is satisfied that she understands. A melanoma thicker than a millimetre trends to bad news and escalates the chance of spread and metastasis. All of Christine's previous cancerous growths have been just under a millimetre. All of them caught early because of their shared vigilance.

Dave's Sorel boots crunch on the pavement, which is

hard-packed with snow left behind by the plow and flattened by cars. They don't have a sidewalk on their street, something they both find odd considering the school on the corner. Darkness signals the street lights to glow. He reaches the first house, four doors down from their own place. As he approaches, he can see a woman with short grey hair standing at a sink in a brightly lit kitchen. He recognizes her as one of the dogwalkers, someone he has waved to and said hello. He rings the bell, an old-school ding dong so loud he can hear it from his side of the door. He waits. No answer. It wouldn't be polite to ring a second time, he decides, before turning away to retrace his steps down the few squares of salted, shovelled asphalt back to the street. He doesn't look up or back to see if the woman is still at the sink.

He skips a few homes, decides to try the house across the street. At least he knows their names. The man Dave recognizes as Phil answers, wearing a plaid flannel shirt and baggy blue sweatpants.

"I'm Dave from across the street," says Dave.

"Right," says Phil. He opens the door a bit wider and gestures for Dave to come in. He stomps his boots, steps onto a heavy-duty floor mat. This is his first time in the house.

"I'd like to talk to you about snow clearing," Dave says. "If you have a minute."

"You want to complain to our councillor. Done it, Dave. And still, terrible service."

"No, I mean the driveways."

"Oh," says Phil. "We've already hired someone to take care of that."

"No, not that. I was thinking about a snowblower."

"You want to buy my old snowblower?"

"No, Phil. I was thinking that we, a few neighbours, could

chip in and buy a new snowblower. Together, as a group. Take turns using it."

Dave hasn't been invited any further into the house than the doorway. His pitch is awkward, he realizes, and it is likely too late to recover.

"And I could clear your driveway, no problem," he says. Phil looks down at his faded plaid slippers, crushed in the back where he jams in his feet, and Dave is afraid his offer is an insult.

"Leave it with me," Phil finally says before he closes the door.

At the next house, a woman named Jan Matthews answers the door within seconds, almost as if she had been expecting him. When she had a broken arm last summer, he'd lifted a heavy "For Sale" sign into the trunk of her SUV, her first and last name in bold black letters at the bottom.

Jan gestures him into her tiled foyer with a wide smile and says, "Oh, Dave. You live across the way. With Christine, yes?"

Dave launches into his spiel. This pitch goes better, he feels, than the last one. Jan listens, asks a reasonable question—where would the machine be stored—nods at appropriate moments.

At the end, though, she tells him that while Dave has a wonderful proposal—innovative, very green— she prefers that her son shovel the driveway.

"So important to develop a strong work ethic in young people, isn't it, Dave?"

"Of course," he replies, unable to recall ever having seen a young man shovelling the driveway. After a snowfall it goes uncleared for days, and the snow tires of Jan's buffed Audi sink into icy ruts. One time, Dave couldn't help himself and sneaked over while she was out. He spent an hour chipping and clearing the hardened snow with his own shovel, and threw down handfuls of road salt.

"Here's my info," Jan says now, handing him an embossed business card.

"I have contacts all over this street, Dave. I'll ask around."

After two more unanswered doorbells, Dave aborts his mission, for the night at least. His timing is wrong, he reasons. Too late, too dark, too cold. They may see his proposal differently on a bright Saturday morning. Maybe.

Christine is waiting at the door when he gets home, sitting on the bottom of the stairs. He almost walks into her. She puts a finger to her lips and gestures to follow her to their bedroom. Dave struggles with his snow boots, goes up with his jacket still on.

"1.9 millimetres," she says into the hallway light that seeps into the darkened bedroom. She reaches their bed, turns on her bedside lamp.

"Thicker than the edge of a penny, doctor said, but not a nickel yet. Lymph node biopsy tomorrow."

He envelopes her, pulls her close to his cold jacket.

"Even if this turns out okay, we'll just have to deal with it again," she says into his shoulder. "It's something in me."

Later, he checks his phone calendar, planning to cancel any other commitments for tomorrow. The date is familiar. Same day as their mortgage renewal, he realizes, which crept up without either of them noticing, and will flip them at midnight into an open term with a loan shark interest rate and a ballooning payment.

DAVE SITS ON an uncomfortable chair in the "small procedure" waiting room at the hospital, phone to his ear while

Christine has a lymph node, or several lymph nodes, sliced up, or maybe sliced out, he really isn't clear. A soothing, AI-generated female voice claims the bank is experiencing higher-than-normal call volumes. He hopes to gather information about their options, if there are any.

As he waits, he studies photos of his wife's rear end on his phone. Sees a multi-toned splotch with uneven, jagged edges. Asymmetrical, the left side darker and—he can still feel the strange texture—rough under his winter-dry fingers. The right side, flat, the skin a mottled reddish brown. Compares the twin photos, a futile exercise, to calculate if the splotch is larger in the second picture, which he shot just a few days after the initial photo, the same day they went to the dermatologist.

The skin on Christine's ass was supposed to be his responsibility. She had entrusted it to him for safekeeping. Had he missed this? Or had a random spark ignited between monthly inspections, the cells going rogue and multiplying like a wildfire? There were only two possibilities.

The automated call centre voice thanks him for his patience. It warns that if he hangs up now, he'll lose his place in line.

He shoves the phone in his pocket as Christine rounds the corner, wearing a thick turtleneck and parka. She balls up a hospital gown and throws it in a laundry bin. He can't see a wound dressing but knows it's under there somewhere.

ON THE FIRST day in May, the real estate agent from down the street, Jan Matthews, tours their home. She arrives at the door with a pink and white Sobeys bouquet, wearing a floral blouse in similar colours. They haven't committed to listing with her, or with anyone, but she hadn't been openly rude about the snowblower so Dave wants to give her a shot. The agent follows Christine from room to room, Dave trailing behind. She is impressed by the neutral paint colour, a warm grey.

"Revere Pewter?" Jan asks.

Christine says, "No idea. Previous owners."

"The people with the insurance business," says Jan. "I didn't really know them."

"Oh, really," says Christine.

Jan compliments the hardwood floors, the updated kitchen with its shiny appliances and deep pot drawers. None of it chosen by Christine or Dave. Hunted down, mulled over, selected, and paid for by people they know only as names on a stack of legal documents plastered with yellow "sign here" stickies.

Jan stands in the middle of Dave and Christine's bedroom, halfway between the window overlooking the driveway and the window facing the backyard.

"Four bedrooms upstairs," she says. "We call this a unicorn house. Rare!"

Christine and Dave's almost-grown children are onside with a sale. They claim they don't care. They didn't grow up in this bougie neighbourhood. None of them, they say, understood why their parents bought the house with pinky-beige vinyl siding in the first place.

The tour continues. Jan also loves the multi-level deck; it will be a great selling feature.

"Everyone wants to maximize their outdoor space, don't they?"

In the attached garage, Jan admires the hooks and shelves, the bike racks. "Fabulous storage," she says. Dave looks at the bare corner he'd prepared for the snowblower.

He doesn't feel a pang, feels nothing but relief. Now he won't need to trudge house-to-house to explain the change in plans. In the end, it was a mild winter anyway. They got through it and his old shovel worked just fine.

After the tour, they talk business in the afternoon sun of the living room. Jan suggests they remove most of their belongings and stage the house with modern, fashionable furniture she can provide as part of her full-service sales package. Dave watches Christine, decides to take his cue from her. He expects she will reject this calculated depersonalization of her home.

"We'll see," she says, positioning a coaster on the coffee table before placing a hot mug of coffee in front of the agent.

"If we do all of that, what's a realistic sale price? How much do you think we can get?"

The number that Jan quotes, a conservative estimate she claims, is $242,000 more than they paid for the house twenty-eight months ago.

"Interesting," says Christine, sipping her coffee.

Dave sees exactly where this is going. She feigns composure but there's a light in Christine's eyes, energy that screams *List This Fucking Millstone*. Insist on a closing date that suits their schedule. If this is supposed to be such a sellers' market, why not, for once in your life, negotiate maximum control over the entire process? Accept this pile of completely unearned money, then bank the cash, pay off some debt and find somewhere to wait it out, get a little breathing room.

"You'll buy again?" asks the agent—greedy, or maybe just hwopeful—Dave senses, for a double commission.

Christine looks at him quickly, a micro glance, and an even smaller side movement of her head. Then she says: "We're unsure at the moment."

But this isn't quite true. They do have a plan.

After they sell, they are going to rent her eighty-nine-year-old aunt's condo in the city's North End. It is a sprawling, dated, three-bedroom apartment with floral wallpaper and pink shag carpet, even in the bathroom.

They have it all worked all out with Christine's cousins, Darlene and Mike. Things are coming together. After sixteen months on a waiting list, their mother moved into a nursing home last week. The cousins insist they won't put the apartment on the market until the old lady dies.

"Nothing permanent, you know," Darlene had said. "But for the next little while, or however long, better you guys than total strangers."

Dave and Christine know the aunt could hang on for years or be gone in weeks. Or that the cousins could just change their minds and sell, any time. Any of this is possible. They're aware there are no perfect solutions, but this arrangement is real, at least for now.

Jan looks concerned.

"So you really don't know what you're going to do?"

She gently taps Christine's arm as she places a short stack of paper in front of her.

"You know I'm here for you, whatever you two decide. Just be careful. It's tricky out there right now, especially when you're on the other side, trying to find something."

Dave watches as one of his wife's freckled hands flips through the sheets. The other one repeatedly pushes blonde hair away from her face. This is a tic that pops up when she's anxious, especially when she denies being anxious.

He wonders if fresh growths have sprouted or are festering right now on the scalp beyond her hairline. After Jan leaves, he'll suggest they examine the area a few weeks ahead of schedule. Christine can survey the front, and Dave will scour the back.

"We really appreciate all of this," he says and smiles at Jan.

She's been a decent enough neighbour, after all. And he hopes she will be good—very good—at her job.

"There's just a lot to consider," he adds. "And what we're trying to do right now is keep all of our options open."

Gap Year

SANDRA SHADOWS HER DAUGHTER EMMA ACROSS EUROPE. Whenever Emma makes a move, her mom sneaks along too. Sometimes Sandra scoots ahead and pops into museums or tourist sites before her daughter has crossed a real border into a new country. Sometimes she attempts to be a local guide.

"Are you following me or, like, going ahead of me? It's getting creepy."

Emma said this a few weeks ago, after her mother texted her links for the five best wine bars within a one-mile radius of the top-rated youth hostel in Edinburgh.

"Of course not, sweetie. I'm just being supportive."

Sandra reasons that since her virtual visits are no secret from Emma, or mostly no secret, they can't be considered surveillance.

"That would be weird. I'm just excited to see you experience so much, so young, and I'm so happy for you."

"Can you stop lurking then, please? Or at least don't tell me about it."

THIS FRIDAY MORNING, Sandra sips unsweetened chamomile tea at her laptop, one of the few people in the office before the May long weekend. She scrolls through the website for the Amsterdam youth hostel where Emma plans to spend the weekend with other teaching assistants she has met in Lyon. The job pays €900 a month plus room and board. For that, Emma helps a high school English teacher twelve hours a week, gets seven weeks of paid vacation, and doesn't work on Mondays. Money in her pocket and a schedule that leaves plenty of time to travel.

Must be nice, Sandra says with a smile to her condo neighbours, to the guy who runs the coffee shop in the office lobby, to the fill-in doctor who reluctantly renewed her sleeping pill prescription.

Sandra and Emma see each other on FaceTime every Tuesday night. A Friday morning call is unusual, but Sandra's cell buzzes at seven o'clock, which is lunch hour in France. Sandra taps "accept" three times before it takes and Emma's thin face fills the phone screen.

"I can't find my passport. I seriously tore my room apart looking for it. It's gone, Mom. Gone."

Sandra gets up and kicks her office door closed.

"That's fixable, sweetie."

"We're supposed to fly tonight."

"Plans don't always work out. The tickets were super cheap, right?"

Emma twirls a strand of hair. She has an idea.

Could Sandra please go home and find the emergency copies of Emma's birth certificate and passport? Can her mom scan and email them? Like, this morning? Then she'll rush to the embassy.

"I guess you never did take pictures of them like I suggested," says Sandra.

"Please, Mom."

"I'll see what I can do."

When Emma disappears, her mother turns back to images of the Dutch hostel, billed as a two-minute walk from the Van Gogh Museum.

"All the little touches to make your stay more enjoyable," the Hostel Van Gogh claims, as sun streams across the crisp white linens of four narrow bunk beds. In another photo, there's a mural wall of Vincent, his scruffy red moustache and beard framing a scowl. He peeks across a row of tables in the hostel's ultra-modern cafeteria, overseeing a group of young people playing cards and eating snacks. Their backs turned away from him. Laughing.

Kids like Emma, never away from home before. She used to be so anxious that she clung to Sandra at airport security. Now, she casually mentions a forty-euro return ticket to fly to Porto or Torino for the weekend. And the high-speed train that can whip her to Paris in a few hours on a youth fare.

Last night, by text, she announced that she will not be coming home any time soon.

Signed on for yr. 2!

what? pls call what about school?

Sandra minimizes the computer screen. The monitor and keyboard are the only items on her desk. The desk occupies most of the office, but Sandra has squeezed in a side table where she displays Emma's high school graduation photo and a dish of Dollar Store candies for guests. She reaches into her lunch bag for a muffin. Why not have a bite to eat and another tea before racing home to fetch her daughter's papers? Sandra knows exactly where they are, stored in a locked briefcase with her life insurance policy and her will.

She steps out of her office and walks a gauntlet of empty cubicles to get to the break room. Desks have been abandoned as people make it a four-day weekend.

The office wraps around the elevators and bathrooms. The telecom company has rules about workspaces. Most people spend their day in a cubicle of eight square feet, with a single coat hook and an eighteen-inch cabinet for personal items. The cubicles are snug up against four walls of windows. In the middle are managers' offices that mirror Sandra's, which has a door but no window, and glass walls.

Only one office has it all: a door, real walls, and a window with a grand view of Halifax Harbour. There's no entry to the corner suite without an upgraded swipe card or an invitation.

The boss's office is empty this morning, and it is so quiet Sandra hears a tiny squeak with each step of her casual-day suede sneakers on the thin commercial carpet.

SANDRA'S ASSISTANT, NICOLE, was supposed to hike the Blomidon trail today with her boyfriend and picnic on a cliff overlooking Minas Basin. That was the plan, but when Sandra asked her to "help hold down the fort" instead, Nicole agreed. Her temporary contract is up for renewal.

Nicole is dumping old coffee grounds as her boss comes into the kitchen. She asks after Emma, where she plans to visit next. Sandra is always primed for show and tell, so Nicole settles in for a detailed description of Emma's school break on the Greek island of Santorini. Invests in the obligatory oohhs and ahhs as they linger over pictures of white-washed buildings and the shimmering, black sand of the beaches. The sun-bleached hair of the girls on a hike up to the island's volcano.

"Whatever they feel like doing, they do, and whenever they want to pick up and go, they go," says Sandra.

"A volcano. Cool," says Nicole, pouring a carafe of water into the coffee maker.

A volcano possibly still active, Sandra has read.

Nicole positions her mug and presses the brew button.

And now Emma is off to Amsterdam.

"Did you know they have boutique hostels now?"

"Do they?" says Nicole, watching the coffee drip into her mug.

"Flat screen TV, Wi-Fi. Croissants and cappuccino, makeup mirrors. Private bathrooms. Air conditioning." Sandra laughs as she unwraps a tea bag. "God forbid anyone is uncomfortable."

"God forbid," says Nicole.

SHORTLY AFTER EIGHT-THIRTY, Sandra's cell vibrates.

any progress?

She pockets the phone and circles the perimeter of the floor, opting for the long way back to her office and saying hello along the way to the handful of people who showed up today. She passes by their co-op work term student, who started last week and immediately volunteered to organize an 2SLGBTQI+ awareness session. She's sorting out the agenda and doesn't see Sandra coming. The student's name isn't posted on her cubicle yet, so Sandra says, "Hey there."

The young woman looks up and smiles. "Hi."

"Don't let me interrupt," says Sandra and moves on.

Then she passes by Frank Warner, who had promised to retire but reneged. On the strength of a proposal with vague wording, he's hanging around for an extra year to come up with ideas on to how to attract Generation Z to the workplace.

"Nowhere better to be?" says Frank as he slips his cell into his desk drawer.

"A good day for catch up," says Sandra. "We have a few things to sort out."

He turns on his computer. "Me too."

After she turns away from Frank, Sandra types *working on it.*

thanks xoxo!!!

When Sandra gets back to her office, it occurs to her she really should double-check her email, to be sure she isn't missing something urgent. Someone might need her. First, though, she looks at the Hostel Van Gogh site again. Just a quick peek at its cancellation policy, in case things somehow don't work out for Emma. She gets distracted by a link to the Van Gogh Museum offering a "browse through the collection."

As Sandra looks at one of the famous paintings—those sunflowers—someone bangs on her glass wall. Cindy, the cleaner, is here to collect garbage.

She's chatty today, still glowing with memories of a Las Vegas vacation. It was supposed to be a getaway with a new boyfriend but her son, her sister, her brother, and his wife decided to come along.

"Bunch of lunatics," Cindy says. "But what the hell."

The first morning in Vegas, Cindy grabbed a Bloody Mary from the breakfast buffet and plunked down at a slot machine. She won fifty dollars on her first try. Then another fifty. And then two hundred. Cindy stuck to the same machine and the winning streak continued for three days. She came home with everyone's plane tickets covered and an extra $1,300.

"You've been there, right?" says Cindy, emptying Sandra's recycling box.

"No," Sandra replies, she has never been to Vegas. "I don't gamble."

"There's lots else to do," Cindy tells Sandra, who had warned before the trip that the house always wins.

"We saw the desert from the Eiffel Tower. Vegas has a real Eiffel Tower."

"But smaller than the real, real one, right?" says Sandra.

She decides not to add, "My daughter has been to the real one. Twice."

It is important to be tactful in these situations.

It is not as if Sandra has never been on a plane. She travels—used to travel, anyway—to Toronto once a year for human resources meetings. They used to hold sessions across the country but now it's non-stop Zoom, Zoom, Zoom. Once there was a meeting in Vancouver and Sandra stayed for the weekend. She moved from the conference hotel to a bed and breakfast, and spent a whole Saturday exploring the city.

She remembers eating a warm croissant at Stanley Park, looking out at English Bay. The waters were motionless and although she was alone, she did not feel lonely.

Sandra's cell rings. Cindy pushes her cart out the door and past the next glass office, which is locked and empty, and past the next, also unoccupied today, and so on down the line.

It's Sandra's ex-husband, Neil, so she lets it go to voicemail. Her daughter has told her, almost proudly, that he messages her every night just to check in. Emma says she reads his note every morning. Together they've built an unbroken chain of WhatsApp messages across the Atlantic Ocean.

Excessive, thinks Sandra. He's smothering the girl.

Sandra and Neil have been separated for about eleven months. Married twenty-four years, they had a backyard wedding two weeks after college graduation.

The sex ended four years ago. Neither of them can pinpoint how or why. Inattention, maybe.

"He's lonely," Emma told Sandra a few weeks ago, and said her dad plans to fly over to visit her soon.

"When we were together, the man wouldn't get on a plane. Absolutely refused," Sandra updated Nicole after that call. He was afraid to fly so they took driving holidays—shopping trips to the States or cottage vacations on Prince Edward Island.

This is her version of their choices, the story she repeats to herself and others.

"And now," Sandra said, "look who plans to fly across the Atlantic Ocean."

"Well, that is a bit tricky," said Nicole.

IT's 9:00 A.M. Two o'clock in the afternoon in France.

A FaceTime call comes in from Emma. Sandra watches and listens as eleven rings come and go.

Time to tackle email. Not much there. Colleagues across the country are racing to cottages or campgrounds. They're prepping barbecues for family meals, meeting friends for espresso martinis on restaurant patios. Since there's nothing begging for her attention, it seems like a good opportunity to clean out her inbox. Sandra organizes it by file size and then makes decisions. Delete, store, or flag for the future. She has a productive half-hour and whips through more than two hundred messages.

Turning back to her phone, she listens to Neil's voicemail. He was phoning about his trip to see Emma, to check dates in case Sandra also plans to visit. When Emma first told Sandra about his upcoming trip, she'd called her ex and said, "You're going to France? Really?"

"Why not?"

"Twenty-four years and we go nowhere and now you suddenly have the travel bug?"

"Lighten up," Neil laughed, not unkindly, but he did laugh.

"Get a passport. Go. What's stopping you?"

What Neil doesn't know is that she does have a passport, and it's not her first. Even before you needed a passport to go to the States, she'd owned one. Each time they drove across the border to shop or go to a ball game, she was ready. But no one ever asked to see it and her first passport expired, unused. She applied for a new one when Emma went to France. It's tucked, hidden really, under a pile of winter socks in her bottom drawer.

Sandra deletes Neil's message and texts Emma: *Technical problems...hang on!*

Then she returns to her oversized computer screen and methodically runs through a stack of employee grievance files, adding notes to brief her boss for union meetings. After twenty years, Sandra sees a predictable pattern. If only a manager had handled things differently, intervened at the right time, done the right thing or the kind thing, compromised a little, tried to bridge the gap, these employees would likely never have filed complaints. Things would never have deteriorated too far to salvage.

BY THE TIME she finishes her notes it's almost eleven in the Atlantic time zone.

mommy do u need help...is all okay

The Canadian embassy in Lyon has likely locked its doors for the weekend. Emma might miss out on Amsterdam with her friends but that's not the end of the world, is it? She'll have other opportunities. Plenty of them. That's why she's over there.

Kids of that age have no perspective, Sandra thinks, so Emma will likely be a bit disappointed. Maybe angry.

I'll tell her I was stuck in an emergency meeting. An employee threatened another employee and we had to sort it out.

I'll tell her I tripped and hit my head but don't worry I'm fine. Just a bump.

I'll tell her I had a fender bender.

The flashing dots on her phone alert her that Emma is typing. A new text comes in:

Found it! Forgot hid in laundry bag ha ha...

sorry trouble mommy xoxoxoxo

Sandra has cried at work before, but normally she can make it to a bathroom one floor below or above. She never cries on this floor, in this glass room. This time, though, there isn't time to escape. The tears come quick and hard. She swivels, turning her body away from the front. Her head almost hits the grey plaster behind her desk.

Sandra sobs with her entire body. She shakes with the power of it. But the weeping is oddly soundless—there is no wailing, no keening, no howling. She hunches in her ergonomic chair. Her torso shakes and her nose overflows with watery snot. A violent cry, to be sure, but silent. There is barely a whimper beyond the necessary gulping, sniffing, and breath-catching.

Even before she cries herself out, before she blows her nose for the umpteenth time, she already senses what should happen next. She should touch up her lipstick and get back out on the floor. She knows what the right thing to do would be. She should graciously inform Nicole, what's-her-name the student, and even Frank Warner that they can all leave early.

"Go now. Don't waste the day," she intends to say. "I'm okay on my own."

That would be the correct move.

EMMA POSTS A dozen photos on Instagram over the weekend. There she is at a café in the middle of a crowd of young people. Glasses and bottles hoisted in the air. One of the guys, dark wavy hair falling across his face, has his arm around her. His eyes are on Emma, not the camera. She appears completely unaware that she is the focus of his attention.

More shots follow. Canals, bikes, tulips, smiles. Everybody is having the time of their life.

Sandra is already editing, choosing the pictures she will show Nicole and a few other colleagues. One of the women, a manager about Sandra's age, will sigh dramatically and say "that kid is living our life" and they'll all laugh before heading back to their desks with their thermal coffee mugs and reusable water bottles.

Sandra studies these photos Monday night, alone in bed in her 850-square-foot condo. Her laptop rests on a pale lavender comforter as she finishes a bottle of Provençal rosé. Then she flips to the Van Gogh Museum again, clicks on "Virtual Visit."

After whizzing through the landscapes and flowers and peasants, Sandra pauses at *Van Gogh's Chair*. Her fingers hover over the laptop's track pad; the painting disturbs her. Vincent isn't in the picture, he's absent but has left his pipe and tobacco on the straw seat of a plain chair. The tiled floor is bare. The chair, it seems to Sandra, is blocking the door. He painted this, she reads, while hosting Paul Gauguin for nine weeks in a yellow house with green shutters in the village of Arles.

Sandra tilts the bedside bottle to pour the last of the pale pink wine, and moves on to Vincent's self-portraits. The notes explain that he posed in front of a mirror, turning back and forth from the canvas to his reflected image. How could he bear it, she wonders, through all those years and all those attempts?

To endlessly scrutinize yourself like that, like this, it is not normal.

She hits the "next" button repeatedly. The images flow together like a time-lapse video or an old-fashioned flipbook. Five years of Vincent's life animate and unspool in less than a minute.

Beard. No beard.

Pipe. No pipe.

Straw hat. Felt hat. Hatless. A bandage where the ear used to be.

His head rotates right to left and back again. While the image shifts and morphs with each click, Vincent's gaze fixes firmly on Sandra. He follows her until the end, his eyes transforming from green to grey, evading her, looking beyond.

Is This My Christine?

CHRISTINE AND I WERE BEST FRIENDS, FOR A TIME, IN JUNIOR high. We were tight, practically inseparable. My sister, Clare, knew her too but I wouldn't say they were close, not in the same way. I haven't seen or heard from Christine in four decades but she comes back into my head in the middle of my first Al-Anon meeting. I don't know, maybe it's the venue, a church basement.

Going to Al-Anon is a gesture of love for Clare. She is living with us, temporarily. When she suggested I switch my Ashtanga class to another night to spend Tuesday evenings at meetings for families of drinkers, I did it without complaining. I would feel incredibly guilty if I did not attend and I absolutely should attend.

But I don't buy into their three Cs: Didn't *Cause It. Can't Control It. Can't Cure It.*

How about someone sure as hell did cause it. How about prove that I couldn't have prevented it. How about should have helped, could have fixed it. Should have known, would have found a way.

If it makes people feel better to wash themselves clean of responsibility—lather rinse repeat—to self-absolve, then fill your boots. But could anyone in my situation believe that?

For god's sake, Clare is my baby sister. Woulda coulda shoulda looked out for her is more like it.

I come home from that initial Al-Anon session with questions, not just about Clare and about me but also, inexplicably, about Christine. She hasn't crossed my mind in years, but now I wonder.

It should be easy enough to discover how her life turned out. I start with Google. I search the name we knew her by, Christine Poirier. There's a Christine Poirier mentioned in the Lunenburg, Nova Scotia, obituary of a guy who, by the look of the unfortunate photo, must have died of a massive coronary. This Christine is sister of the deceased and she goes by Poirier-Marchand. My Christine did, I believe, have a brother. I plug her into Facebook to find fifty-eight Christine Marchands. I scroll and scroll and click on the profiles that aren't private. There are non-private Christine Marchands in North Carolina, India, England, Quebec, and Ontario.

But I find one public Christine Marchand in Nova Scotia.

She has a sculpted, blondish bob and poses with a bearded, bald man under a palm-leaf palapa at Playa del Carmen. This Christine wears sunglasses and a floppy hat but from what I can see, appears to be healthy and content and posts inspirational quotes overlaid on sunsets.

It seems as if I'm onto something. I investigate a bit further, find a Facebook page called *Nova Scotia Old Days* where this version of my Christine commented on a vintage photo. Someone had posted a picture of the hippie sandals we all bought for two dollars in the midseventies. We called them "Jesus Christ water walkers" or "buffalo sandals." They were flat slabs of stiff, brown leather with a loop for your big toe, but if you soaked them overnight, the saturated hide moulded to your feet and became part of you.

People in the Facebook group chimed in with memories. The Christine I've settled on writes, "Ha, ha...my old party shoes!"

Clare watches from her favourite spot on my leather sectional, taking refuge under an oversized, hand-knit shawl that I gifted her when she arrived a few weeks ago. She's working through a crossword puzzle in a tattered book she brought from rehab. The house is empty except for us. My husband is out of town for work, and the twins are still in Montreal at McGill.

My sister and I were in different grades but born only eleven months apart. Irish twins, they used to call siblings born the same year. We shared a bedroom in the attic and had three older brothers who mostly ignored us.

"So, are you going to actually friend request her, or just creep?"

WHEN SOME WOMEN marry, they disappear. They change their name, buy a house in the suburbs. Sometimes they move far away. They erase the past: the childhoods they had no control over, their reckless teen years, all the people they slept with —consensual or not. The hungover Saturday brunches with friends, the late-night and early-morning tears. I wonder if that's what happened to Christine. Did she fade into the good life? It would ease my mind, I think, to know.

Clare attempted this vanishing act but her problems stuck. They followed her all the way to Alberta, into marriage and kids and a government job. Followed her so hard she was booted right out of the perfect life. Now she's with me, waiting and hoping for husband number two to take her back, riding out her kids' anger, performing the required penance.

On Mondays and Thursdays she washes her hair, puts on clothes that aren't sweats, and goes to AA.

When she asked me to go to Al-Anon, she said, "You're convinced you're the good sister in this scenario, right? This is what the good sister would do."

I ignore the sarcasm and judgment but I refuse to apologize for having a high-functioning marriage, twins succeeding in university, and a comfortable consulting career. Michael and I worked hard, and we earned everything we have.

The night Clare called me and asked to stay with us, it was the first time we'd spoken in months, but I didn't hesitate to say she was more than welcome. She sounded like a little girl on the phone, my baby sister.

"I won't be bad this time," she said. "Promise."

I reassured her. "We'd be happy to have you."

We are fortunate enough to have a proper guest suite with its own bathroom. I bought a new comforter for the queen-sized bed and squeezed my out-of-season clothes into our own walk-in closet to make space for her things. When she arrived, I showed her how to program the bedroom thermostat so she'd be comfortable but I also told her it was okay to open the bedroom window, even with the heat on. I just wanted her to feel at home.

I stocked the fridge and cupboards with her favourite foods, and though we usually keep the sugar in this house to a minimum, I made sure we had chocolate and cookies on hand, because alcoholics, I've read, often have a sweet tooth.

WHEN CHRISTINE AND I were close, she had glossy brown hair parted in the middle, and round blue eyes. We were the core of a revolving group of five or six friends, depending on whose turn it was to be shunned. And Christine never minded if Clare stuck around when we hung out in our basement rec room.

Clare could be a clinger but Christine treated her like an equal. Even painted my sister's nails, gnawed to the quick, with the same frosted polish she wore. She once interrupted a Ping-Pong game to yell instructions through the bathroom door as Clare struggled with a tampon. It had been Christine's idea that Clare should graduate from pads to Tampax, but Clare couldn't manoeuvre one in. Christine finally convinced her to open the door. She held a makeup mirror under her so Clare "could see her parts" and aim accurately.

I stayed outside, bouncing the Ping-Pong ball on the table, but I could hear them giggling.

Christine had no embarrassment. I seethed with it.

She lived in a bungalow with peeling brown paint, a broken fence, and a torn window screen. The house was a few doors down from St. Augustine's Church and parish hall. Her father was a bus driver and her mother worked at the Sears catalogue counter. Her family wasn't one of the staunch Catholic mega-families who claimed an entire row at Sunday mass. They were Easter and Christmas people, if that.

She was the type of friend your parents always felt virtuous about having over for supper because it made them feel like they were doing a good deed.

"Who knows what goes on in that house?" my mother once said after sending Christine home with leftover chocolate chip cookies.

Friday nights, we all went to youth club at the church hall. The guys would play basketball or floor hockey, and we would sit on the stage watching them, our legs hanging down. Father Riley would usually wander in to say hello. He was barely out of the seminary, junior to the old Monsignor who droned on every Sunday. We thought he looked like Luke Skywalker.

The youth club was his territory, his idea.

WE STARTED DRINKING the summer after grade eight. Three or four of us would share a six-pack of brown, stubby bottles of Schooner or Keith's. Someone's older brother's scuzzy friend would go to the liquor store for five bucks and meet us in the school field with the beer stashed in an Adidas bag.

Christine was the only one with the guts to sneak liquor from her own home. She'd water down her parents' quarts of vodka and rum, and create concoctions in half-empty Coke bottles.

"I know all their hiding places," she claimed.

One Friday night in late June, the summer before high school, something happened that I wonder about today. It was youth club night. It wasn't dark yet when Christine appeared with three basketball players in the church parking lot. The sun hadn't even set but, already, she could barely walk. One of the guys was her boyfriend, Danny. He was holding her up and he looked scared.

"I found her like this," he said. "On her front steps."

Danny had been the cutest guy we knew until midway through eighth grade. He had curly dark hair and soft brown eyes. He looked normal before Christmas, but after the break his face was covered in volcanoes of pus. Some of the eruptions were three inches wide, covering most of a cheek. But he was the smartest and funniest boy in the class, and the tallest, so he managed to maintain his popularity for a while, as if his condition was temporary, like the flu. But it intensified, spreading like a blight to his neck, shoulders, and back.

Lesions the size of plums poked out from his basketball singlet. Danny's efforts in that polyester uniform only irritated his affliction. Sweat poured over the boils and pustules on his body.

As winter went on and the festering sores persisted, we figured Christine would dump him. But she stuck even closer.

I remember her saying she'd lick his face when they made out.

"Because I love him," she said, cutting out skin care articles and ads from *Seventeen* magazine.

We all believed it.

She dabbed tinted Clearasil on his cysts until they looked like shiny pink balls and she haunted the aisles of the drugstore and questioned the pharmacist, bought antiseptics, astringents, green bottles of Phisohex. But his malady was beyond cure. The poison oozed from within, and nothing could change that.

He tried too: He went to a doctor who burned off lesions and radiated his tender skin. He took medicine that made him look acid-scorched. Nothing worked, and as he became more disfigured, his popularity faded. By grade ten, he was just another guy with a pitted face and a jean jacket who tried out for the high school basketball team but didn't make it.

He drifted away and no one reached out to bring him back.

Christine floated off in a similar way and no one threw the life ring to her either. In high school she seemed to vanish. I was busy making social inroads with girls from the better parts of town and playing every team sport that would have me. I spotted her a few times hanging around the stoner door with a guy who looked too old for high school. Her once-shiny hair was lank and almost covered her face. I did not say hi.

It was obvious she wasn't with Danny anymore, but I didn't know why or when they broke up. They were both out of my circle now, beyond my attention.

That summer night in the parking lot, she was wearing jeans and a pastel T-shirt. Stumbling in circles on wobbly Jell-O legs. Danny looking frightened as he tried to keep her upright. Father Riley came out of the manse wearing a white T-shirt and black pants. His face was flushed, his hair damp and sticky. He stood silently on the edge of our group, but when people noticed him, they stepped back. Danny released Christine's hand and retreated too, leaving her alone, staggering around the perimeter.

The priest made his way closer to Christine.

"Poor Tina," he said. "Teeny, tiny Tina."

He always called her Tina although no one else did. He had pet names for the ones he liked, guys and girls.

Christine wagged a finger. "Where's your costume?"

"Tina," said Father Riley. "You're not feeling well."

He told us to bring her inside the church hall and take her to the cloakroom outside the girls' bathroom.

"I think maybe she has the flu," he said.

We arranged her on the floor, back against the wall, and she was wasted enough to go along with it. Danny tried to come in but the priest waved him away. Then he sent me to the church hall kitchen for a big glass of water. I did what I was told. At that time, we all did what we were told, or maybe that's the way I choose to remember it.

Father Riley took the water from me and held the cup to Christine's lips.

"Tina, drink this."

She pushed away the glass with her short, pink nails. Then she looked him directly in the eye.

"Poor Tina," she said, mimicking him. "Drink this, poor, poor Tina."

Then she laughed, loud and sarcastic and hard.

No one did this. Laughing at a priest, directly into his face, but Father Riley didn't seem angry. He didn't even look disappointed. He offered the glass again. He was crouching now.

"Water helps."

This time she opened her lips as if to comply but then let the liquid dribble out of the corners of her mouth.

The priest stood up and handed me the cup.

"You girls keep an eye on her," he said before he slipped out the door.

We figured she'd puke but she didn't, not that night or any night I can recall. And though she was just one hundred yards from her own house, no one suggested taking her home. After I took my turn sitting with her, I went into the gym to watch the guys play basketball.

No one told her parents or our parents. The secret was locked down. I don't recall the details, but Christine must have slept over at someone's house, where she could safely blend into a crowd of six or eight or ten siblings.

That would make sense, right?

TWO DAYS LATER we went to the manse to play junior bookkeeper, as we did every Monday night. My mother volunteered the three of us—me, Christine, and Clare—and we kept track of the money from the collection envelopes. My mother made me bring Clare along because Monday was also her bridge night and Christine didn't seem to mind, but to me, the parish house always smelled stale and I wished I was home watching one of our two TV channels.

Parish families picked up a box of the year's envelopes in January. The men in charge of the collection stacked the labelled boxes on a table just inside the church doors. If no one picked up your family's box for weeks, well, that was evidence of something. If you didn't even have family envelopes, people watched you drop naked bills into the basket, or worse, loose coins.

"You can't force people to do what they don't want to do," my mother would say.

But she was surrounded by rows of people—her own children even—who would have preferred to be asleep or anywhere else. Our parents were oblivious, or maybe they paid attention to the wrong things. Maybe we all did.

By Monday night, the actual cash and cheques were already dealt with. Our job was just to transfer the numbers from the envelope faces into a ledger.

We three girls would gather in the manse's meeting room. Father Riley would dump a blue velvet sack of empty white envelopes onto an oak table. Christine sorted alphabetically, Clare read out the names and amounts, and it was my job to record everything. At age fourteen we knew how much, how often. If you drove to church in a brand new Impala but only shoved in two bucks, we knew. We also knew who wrote cheques for ten dollars or more every week. I'm sure some of those cheques bounced but we had no way of knowing.

While we did our accounting job, the ancient Monsignor was nowhere to be found: his spare time was a blank that we weren't curious about. Father Riley would greet us at the door, pile on the work, and leave us to it. But sometimes he popped in with treats. It was unpredictable when he would shine his light. He would randomly appear and throw bags of stale Halloween chips on the table, their blue foil bright against the paper envelopes. Sometimes he unloaded unwanted baking from the ladies of the parish who tempted his sweet tooth—dry oatmeal cookies with raisins, overly sugary date squares, crumbly tea biscuits: we ate it all.

I ADMIT I might be creating a story where there is none. Maybe I'm trying to solve a mystery or a puzzle that does not exist. We're built to demand reasons and assign blame. If something bad happens, it must be somebody's fault. They say hindsight is 20/20 but you can only remember what you notice and your mind can be pretty picky about that too.

THE MONDAY AFTER Christine was so wasted at youth club, we three were quieter than usual as we recorded the collection numbers. Christine didn't mention what happened on Friday night and I didn't ask. I cannot say why.

After a while, Father Riley came in with a shoebox. He said he had a present for us, a token of appreciation. He dug into the box and handed us each a clunky chain, not gold or silver but a dull, grey metal that looked like it would make your skin itch or turn your neck green. There was a painted medallion on each necklace. Not exactly a teenage girl's dream jewellery, but here was this priest telling us we were special.

He gave Clare a Saint Nicholas medal. Mine said *Saint Christopher* along the top and *Protect Us* on the bottom. In the middle, there was a picture of an old guy with a walking stick, carrying baby Jesus on his back.

You'd think Father would have picked the Saint Christopher medal for Christine but he handed her Saint Ursula.

"Patron saint of schoolgirls, Tina," he said.

We weren't sure what to say or do. Clare immediately put hers around her neck, I held mine in my hand, and Christine shoved hers into her pocket. When I went home, I felt guilty I hadn't traded so she could have her namesake. Extra guilty, because I still had no clue where she'd slept on Friday night.

The following Monday, Father Riley answered the door looking as if he'd just woken up. He wore a faded white shirt and gripped a half-empty Pepsi bottle. He dumped the envelopes out of the velvet bag, sat down, and planted his bare feet up on the table. I didn't mean to stare but his dirty soles were directly in my line of sight.

He asked if we had shown our parents the gifts. I looked to Christine: she looked down and started sifting through the envelopes. I nodded yes.

"Our mother says it was very thoughtful," said Clare.

"I bet," said the priest, and Clare turned fifty shades of red. She hadn't yet become an expert liar.

He leaned back in the leather chair and told us a story. Turns out the saint medals were leftovers, just like the Halloween chips. They weren't supposed to sell them to parishioners anymore because Rome had downgraded these saints a few years back. Their supposed miracles had been officially debunked, no longer miraculous enough.

"Demoted, girls," he said, and emptied his bottle.

"And this Saint Ursula, that was maybe the best one."

There are different versions of this tale, but I guess she supposedly led a cult of eleven thousand medieval virgins. Facing an unwanted marriage to a pagan king, she escapes and goes on a religious pilgrimage to Rome with thousands of these young girls following her. On the journey, though, Ursula rejects another proposal from, you guessed it, another pagan king, only this time, the second guy goes crazy and slaughters her and all her innocent handmaidens. That's it.

"Hard to believe they ever bought that story in the first place, isn't it?" Father Riley said, crossing his feet on the table.

Christine didn't even look up while he spoke. Instead, she concentrated on organizing the mess of envelopes into orderly, alphabetical stacks. Then she handed Clare the first envelope to read out. Business as usual.

After that, Christine stopped coming with us to the manse, claiming she'd found a regular Monday night babysitting gig. I kept on through the summer and used the beginning of high school as my own excuse to stop. It wasn't any fun without Christine.

I think I only saw her a few times that summer. Her Monday night gig became a summer job, and I was a junior day camp counsellor at the YMCA. I didn't phone her and she didn't call me. Or maybe she phoned and I didn't call back.

I wish I knew for sure.

Clare and a few other girls took over the church envelopes. Our mother thought it would be good for her, and Clare wasn't the type to disagree. She and her friends hung out at the youth club like we had, and, of course, there was always an older guy to go to the liquor store for them. I thought nothing of it; this seemed to be the natural order of things.

Father Riley disappeared that summer, blowing out of our lives as quickly as he had blown in. Clare and I eavesdropped on Mom telling Dad that the priest had been sent away after he showed up dead-drunk at a wedding rehearsal. Someone told her he'd yelled at the organist to "shut the eff up." The mother of the bride was a first cousin of the archbishop, so all it took was one phone call.

"There's a place in Florida where they send them," we overheard our mother say.

CLARE AND I linger over tea and toast. We're cozy, sitting side by side on the living room couch, feet on the glass coffee table. The propane fireplace blazes as February's morning sun streams through our picture window. I'm never not grateful for the abundance of natural light in this room.

It's our last morning before Michael comes home from bank meetings in Toronto, precious time together with no interruptions. Next week Clare returns to Alberta to her maybe ex-husband and kids and employer, to salvage what she can. "Operation Radical Honesty," she's calling it.

I've taken the day off work. Clare immerses herself in her morning crossword while I make my usual rounds on the iPad. Sometimes she looks up from the book and stares out the window. There's not much of a view this time of year, just bare trees. I wonder if she's ruminating about the past or worried about her future.

There's a new class action suit in the news, naming old priests and dead priests. I read the article and announce, "No one we know is on the list."

She puts down the crossword book and swings her legs up on the couch, nudging me with socked feet to make space.

"Why would anyone we know be on that frigging list?"

My sister is particularly snippy today, but I refuse the bait. I try to react to these outbursts with patience and grace. I can't imagine how difficult this must be, to live with her older sister, no home of her own anymore, humiliated and on sick leave from work, estranged from kids and husband, sorting out how to make amends for the crazy and selfish things she did when she was drinking—don't get me started—and trying to avoid temptation all day, every day.

I tell her that Facebook claims St. Augustine's Church and parish hall are on the market. There are online rumours of luxury condos. I've driven by a few times lately. Yesterday, in minus-twenty with a wind chill, I parked the car and peeked through the metal fence that surrounds the property now.

They've already stripped the church down, removed the statues, and dumped them into the parking lot. I guess it's all for sale now if anyone is interested. They covered the Virgin with a blue tarp but not very well, and I watched as the plastic blew around her body in the wind and bitter cold, like she was standing out there in just a skirt.

Father Riley, now just Joe Riley, pops up on the news every now and then, supposedly an advocate for people who live on the street.

"Riley became a social worker," I say to Clare.

I watch her reaction. I have my theories, keep hoping she will confide.

"Imagine," I say. "Think of all those vulnerable people he has access to."

Clare looks at me and shakes her head.

"He's probably sober by now," she says. "And he's just trying to show them that there is a way out. Anyway, a drunk priest doesn't necessarily mean a pervy priest, if that's what you're trying to get at."

I clear our toast plates and put them in the dishwasher. When I get back, I flip my own legs up on the couch so we sit with knees facing and feet touching like when we were kids and we didn't want our brothers to hog the sofa. She rearranges the shawl to cover both sets of legs.

Then I hand her the iPad to show her the Facebook post about the hippie sandals. I've held back for days, but give in because the clock is ticking before she leaves me. I show her the picture of the woman who may or may not be the Christine we knew. My Christine, our Christine. I share my memories of that night in the parking lot, the youth centre, the priest, and the saint medals. Memories that only came back to me since Clare moved in.

I explain that I'm trying to decipher all of this, figure out what it means. My gut tells me there's a connection between the priest and Clare and maybe Christine too. I admit—this is extremely difficult—that I am hoping, maybe even praying, for an aha moment for us, and maybe some forgiveness for me.

"Spare me," she says.

Her hand grips tighter around her mug of green tea. She guzzles this stuff all day, mixing in spoonfuls of honey.

"Stop playing 'My Sister Drinks Because.' Please. Just stop."

Some things are a mystery, she says, and I should accept that. When Clare moved in after rehab, she told me she'd read somewhere that the difference between a mystery and a puzzle is that if you get new information and an answer becomes clearer, then it's a puzzle. But if you get new information and things blur even more, then that's a mystery. This is how she speaks these days.

"But there's still Christine," I say. "We have no idea what happened, or if she was okay that night."

Clare looks at the ceiling and out the window again.

"All right," she says. "There is a story. But I said I wouldn't tell."

I knew it. She claims this is a secret, but I sense she really does need to finally share. It will help her heal. For Clare's own good, I push the old buttons and eventually she spills it.

But she does not tell the story I have in my head. She says something else, about a school dance.

Clare's first week at St. Mike's high school, there was the usual Frosh Week dance. She was nervous and chugged a couple of beers in the parking lot. Inside the school gym, her friends paired off, so she ended up sitting alone on the bleachers. Then Danny, Christine's ex, asked Clare to dance.

"Even I knew he wasn't popular anymore, but I didn't want to embarrass him by saying no."

"Typical you."

"Typical me. It was a slow dance, some Bee Gees crap. But, Jesus, this guy was all over me. Stuck his hand down the front of my jeans. The front."

She put up with it until a liquored Christine appeared. She comes straight and fast across the gym, pushes Danny away, and drags Clare off the dance floor.

"She didn't need to make a scene. But when he saw her, he just took off."

There were rumours floating around in those days about Danny, I remember all this suddenly. The new old information that was always there.

"Okay, so she *saved* you. Where was I during all this?"

"I have no idea. Jesus."

She digs her heel into my forefoot and it hurts.

"Christine took me downstairs to the girls' locker room. It was empty. We sat on the floor and shared the dregs of a pint of vodka and Tang she'd snuck in. She lent me her lip gloss and her comb. She'd just found out that her family was moving to somewhere in Ontario and she was so glad to be leaving."

This part is also new. Did I ever hear that Christine moved away? I can't remember. Maybe, maybe not.

"She says to me, 'Stay away from Danny, he's a frigging dog.' She'd dumped him after he got her drunk on her parents' own liquor before youth club one night. It was blurry and maybe she passed out. She remembered rolling off the couch onto the carpet. He pulled down her pants and made a mess all over her. She had to wipe herself off."

I picture Clare and Christine sitting together on the floor of that dingy locker room, sharing their liquor and their secrets.

"Then it was like it never happened and off they went together to the church hall. He even tied her sneakers for her."

I don't remember anything about that high school dance.

"But I must have been there," I say.

"Irrelevant," says my sister. "What you were doing at the time is not important."

I suspect she's upset because she broke a promise not to tell.

"You're just feeling guilty. Don't feel guilty for telling the truth."

"I do not feel guilty," she says. "And if you care so much about Christine, then go ahead. Reach out. Message this Facebook person."

Clare slurps her tea and puts the mug back on the coffee table, ignoring the hand-painted ceramic coaster that I wish she would use.

She reaches for her crossword, just a few ink-scrawled words away from solving today's puzzle.

"But we both know, right?" she says. "You're never going to do that."

Siesta Key

THEY CATCH THE TUMOUR EARLY AND THE SURGEON MAKES IT disappear. She slices it out and stitches together the sausage ends of Phil Bower's lower colon. For good measure, she also removes a dozen lymph nodes. The biopsy comes back clean.

Dr. Findlay spends just eight minutes with Phil and his wife on discharge day.

"Why can't any of these doctors look people in the eye anymore?" Phil says after she rushes off without a proper goodbye.

"She just seemed worn out to me," his wife, Amelia, says.

Phil is managing okay with his sweatpants and doesn't need her help. He lies on the hospital bed and pulls them up over his butt. She watches as he unties the hospital gown, exposing his chest and the fresh dressings in the space between his groin and belly button.

"What was she? Thirty-five? Forty?"

Amelia throws him the clean T-shirt she brought for the trip home. "No wedding ring," she says, "but that means nothing."

IF YOU ARE a regular at the community theatre in their neighbourhood, you will recognize Amelia. She takes your ticket and greets you at the front door as if she owns the place. Her hair is long and grey. She likes to coil and pile it to make those dangling earrings stand out. At the intermission, she pours your five-dollar merlot into a plastic cup and says, "Isn't the play wonderful."

The Bowers, Amelia and Phil, have been married forty-nine years. Returning home from the hospital, they pull up to the house they should have sold decades ago. They don't need its four bedrooms anymore. Or its three bathrooms and the dusty Ping-Pong table in the basement. Amelia presses the garage door opener on the car shade. An hour later, she settles Phil in a recliner in front of the new, seventy-five-inch flat screen. The TV, his purchase, erases all the surrounding decor. Amelia hands him the remote and he quickly finds a Tiger Woods career retrospective on the Golf Channel.

"All the running around that one did," says Phil as he increases the volume.

"Hungry?" Amelia asks. He shakes his head.

Well, too bad, she decides. He needs to get his strength back. She heads to the kitchen, where she turns up the heat on a pot of carrot-ginger soup and shoves a stick blender into the middle of the mixture. Holds on carefully to the handle as the blades crush the soft vegetables and homemade broth into a puree that will be easier for a recuperating husband to digest.

SHE HADN'T PLANNED a confrontation, wasn't looking for a fight, but when he slurps the final drop of the soup, she cannot help herself. She has been holding back ever since Annie let it slip, accidently on purpose, that her dad came to dinner and whined that he could not afford a new car.

A lie.

And then of course, Annie had blabbed to her brother, Jeff, in Toronto and he'd called Amelia too.

"Now what, Mom?"

But Phil knows damn well that she took only what was hers when she moved out last year, her own money, from her side of the family. She only uses their joint account for groceries and her car payment.

Amelia takes the lunch tray from Phil's lap.

"I heard you told the kids I cleaned you out."

"What? That's not what I said," he says, leaning forward in the recliner, fussing with his fleece throw. It's his favourite, a *Sports Illustrated* gift with subscription. He clutches the blanket and Amelia looks down at her knuckles, knobby and swollen with arthritis, as they grip the tray. She could not force her wedding ring on even if she wanted to. Surely, he realizes if she does officially file papers, does claim her full share, he would still have much more than he needs.

But she hasn't filed papers. She's not sure why. Maybe she'd hoped they could go on for years like this. She would cook Sunday dinner and holiday meals; the grandchildren would set the table. She would scrub the roasting pan after the Thanksgiving turkey and then drive home to her new condo three blocks away. If they both behaved properly, if they kept their priorities in sight, she thought they could keep it together. Live separately without a divorce.

Amelia rattles the tray of dirty dishes, catching herself as the soup bowl almost slides off. "You couldn't help yourself. Couldn't keep your mouth shut. Had to get the kids upset."

"Kids? Jesus, they have grey hair, they're middle-aged."

Phil's own hair has grown wispy. It hasn't been washed for days so the thinning leftovers cling to his head. His body is also thinning; he was a skinny man to begin with and lost more weight with the surgery.

She regrets mentioning his complaints—his lies—about being broke. This isn't the time for another argument. What was she thinking? She has always been able to read him. What does she see now? Someone who needs a nap, not a fight. Well, she can't blame him for that; she's exhausted too. She'll dump the tray in the kitchen, sneak into their bedroom for a nap, and then remake the bed so that he'll never know she was there. Their guest room mattress is awful.

"Forget it, Phil. Sleep. When you wake up, we'll look at your bandage."

Phil presses a button on the recliner and the motor hums gently as his chest falls back and his socked feet are smoothly lifted. He pulls up his blanket and mutes the television. Closes his eyes.

"I'll check that pamphlet they gave us at the hospital. Make sure we're doing everything by the book."

He doesn't answer. Already asleep, maybe.

THEIR SUBDIVISION IS turning over. Young couples are moving into bungalows and tearing down the walls between kitchens, living rooms, and dining rooms. Opening things up. They're putting in skylights to brighten the narrow hallways.

Once, Amelia snooped at an open house at their former next door neighbours' place. It was such fun to drive around the block and park across the street, like a stranger. The house had changed hands, but someone bought to flip, and it was back on the market again nine months later, renovated to look like a magazine cover. The formal dining room where they used to eat lobster Newburg or roast beef with Jack and Louise was now a breakfast bar and family room. Amelia remembers spilling red wine from the oak dining table onto the light beige wall-to-wall carpet. Louise had laughed and said it was no big deal. Not to worry, she'd said, but sprinted to get club soda, and then pursed her lips until their second round of post-dessert liqueur.

That carpet is long gone. It's all hardwood now.

The houses on the Bowers' block are the newest in the neighbourhood. Their home, like the others on this side of the street, perches on a cliff. This isn't for everyone. To build here in the 1980s, they had to hire a geological engineer. The city planning department blessed their blueprints, and then they selected a quality builder who could guarantee that this precariously placed structure would stay put.

To build a house that wouldn't slide down the cliff, would stick for at least fifty years, was an exercise in patience and skill. The payoff was the view: a wall of windows framing evergreens and maples. When the leaves disappear in autumn, a tiny slice of Halifax Harbour reveals itself.

Amelia loves this unexpected glimpse of ocean, the uniqueness of each home that hangs onto the rocky soil on the risk-takers' side of the street. She and Phil chose to build here when others feared the cliff. Apart from insisting on two magnificent decks, she ceded the entire design to him. Phil was an engineer, had the gift of seeing it all in 3-D. This house was his vision come to life, but the moment she stepped through the door into their finished home, Amelia was disappointed. Sure, the view was incredible, but the lay-out triggered claustrophobia and nothing flowed the way it should.

She had never spoken up. What right did she have to complain when she just let it happen, a bystander in her own life?

STANDING WITH THE lunch tray, watching Phil sleep, she thinks about the space between life and death. She could place a burgundy ultra-suede couch pillow on his face and hold it down with two hands.

How long would it take? Would he wake up and struggle, or would his dreams just continue? She isn't religious and believes she is no more or less spiritual than the next person. But she holds in her mind the way she used to feel when she'd smoked some particularly good weed in university, in the few months she was single before pairing off with Phil. She would find a back door, some steps to sit on, or a tree to lie under, and let her mind drift.

Sometimes she would stumble into a moment that made sense of the world. Then the moment would pass.

Annie once asked if she knew anyone who went to Woodstock. She told her daughter that everyone knew someone who knew someone who'd at least tried, but she did not reveal that she went to the bus station by herself and bought a ticket to Moncton, thinking she could figure things out from there.

Then she got off the bus in Truro, bought a hot chicken sandwich and fries at a diner, and waited for the next bus home. She said yes to Phil's proposal the next day.

AMELIA COMES UPSTAIRS from the laundry room with a basket of warm towels and catches him with her phone in his hands. Initially, she kids herself that he's confused, blames the painkillers, but no, that's not it. He must know that she has entered the room, but he keeps scrolling and pressing with thin fingers.

She stops, not wanting to disturb the scene or break the spell. Spies on him while he spies on her. He has likely found a chain of texts.

coffee?

not today maybe tomm

no pressure…just if u want break

"Not much of a writer," he says without looking up.

She does not attempt to retrieve her phone. Instead, she dumps the towels on the couch, sits, and starts to fold.

He will eventually tire of this game. Playing along will only prolong it.

WHEN THEY HAD registered at the hospital, the young woman at the front desk asked if Phil's address was unchanged, the phone number still correct.

"Same family doctor?"

"Yes," he said.

"Next of kin...Amelia Bower?"

"Yes," Amelia answered. "That's me. But I have a new cell number."

Phil looked down at the hands folded in his lap. Age-spotted. Still tanned, despite illness.

AFTER PHIL IS discharged, Annie phones her father every night because her job and her kids mean she can't cross the MacKay bridge more than once a week to help. She calls Phil's cell, not the land line he refuses to give up. Annie is a careful, responsible woman, an economist at the provincial tax department. She has been on her own since her youngest was two, when her ex-husband decided that settling down wasn't his thing.

When Amelia moved out a few years ago, her daughter did not ask why, did not probe. Instead, she kept to the typical script of their conversations. Talked to her mother about the usual things: Work was busy and frustrating, her son had a science project due, and her daughter had strep throat.

"I just wanted something different, you know?" Amelia finally said this one evening before dinner, in response to the unasked question. They were at Annie's place, a slightly cramped townhouse in the not fancy part of Dartmouth.

Her daughter paused briefly.

"I get that," she said. Then she let out a long breath.

"But, sometimes, Mom, I'm not sure you can see it, there is a very thin line between self-actualization and self-indulgence."

"Pardon me?"

"Come on. You left because you could."

Annie pointed at her own walls and floors.

"You left because you had a mortgage-free house and an indexed pension and all the rest of it. Savings and investments."

"You make it sound like we're rich people," Amelia replied. "We're not rich. We're just comfortable."

"Sure," Annie said, "sure."

She tapped her mouth with a closed fist, then added quickly: "I'm sorry, I didn't mean any of that."

"Okay."

"It's just that I'm so tired, Mom, you know? My neck aches and I need to get supper on the table for everyone. I'm sorry."

This time, it was Amelia's turn to pause for a few seconds.

"Don't I deserve to be happy?" she asked.

"Yeah, Mom, sure. I guess. You deserve that."

AMELIA PULLS IN next to Steve's Tacoma in the parking lot for Superstore and the mini-mall. They each roll down a window.

"Hey, sailor," she says. Cringe-worthy, yes, but so what.

"Ready, aye, ready," Steve says, saluting. "Reporting for duty."

He was in the navy before he retired to become a finish carpenter. He's a detail guy in his woodwork but also appreciates the rush of the unexpected, is spontaneous in fun ways. Someone brought him to the neighbourhood theatre to help with the set of last season's musical, and he ended up creating a whole new backdrop no one else had envisioned.

"Look, I only have an hour," says Amelia.

"Okay," he says.

"And I need to go in there for provisions. Says he wants roast chicken tonight."

"Okay. We can just grab a coffee."

Steve jiggles the Bruins key chain hanging from the truck's ignition.

"Or we can go to the flat now and then just run into the store after," he says. "Whatever you want."

He's wearing his jean jacket. Clean-shaven today. He runs a weathered hand through his hair to push back grey waves.

She smiles. "Your place."

"I BOOKED THE CONDO," Phil informs Amelia the next day. He dawdles with his soup. Stir, scoop a half-spoonful from the side, and blow lightly before taking tiny sips. "Could only get a two-bedroom this time. Mailed the deposit."

They rent the Siesta Key condo every February and March, have done for a decade. If you are the type of person who does not see yourself as the type of person who likes Florida, you convince yourself Siesta Key is acceptable because there are no chain hotels, just ten-storey condos for sale or rent, and old-school motels renovated to be retro, right down to the linoleum flooring. The five-mile beach is wide and flat. The quartz sand stays cool underfoot.

Facebook told Amelia that although three of the husbands in their Siesta Key condo group had died in the last eighteen months, their Midwest and Ontario widows were heading down anyway for the sun and the company, and they likely coaxed Phil into doing the same.

The winter group is shifting and reassembling, gliding down to the lower edge of America in a formation that rearranges itself seamlessly.

"Going to fly this time. Rent a car at the airport. Some of them are bugging me to share but I need my own vehicle," Phil says. "Come and go as I please."

"I can't believe they still make people mail cheques," says Amelia.

"The mail still works," he says, mopping up the final drops with one of her tea biscuits. She bakes them but no longer eats them, having gone gluten-free.

"You'd think they'd figure out how to take a credit card by now," she says.

He pushes away his empty bowl. "Mail still does what it's supposed to do. A cheque is still a cheque."

She doesn't envy him his eight weeks with that crowd, but she always enjoyed the Sunday drum circle down on the beach. One evening a week, talented percussionists join the yogis and vegans and belly dancers to lay on a spectacle for tourists and snowbirds. A few couples in Phil and Amelia's group would stroll over to the beach after supper and cocktails.

The Siesta Key drum circle can attract a few hundred people, with a dozen or so serious drummers in the core. Playing congas, bongos, Caribbean steel drums, West African djembes, and goblet-shaped doumbeks and darbukas. Their music has no beginning or end, just a beat that rises and falls, ebbs, and flows. Some musicians are regulars. A Vietnam veteran with a head scarf and a tie-dyed muscle shirt over his leathery form. A dreadlocked white Rasta playing steel drums.

A delicate-boned woman who sits cross-legged, bent over a set of scratched bongos.

And the dancers. A woman who weaves across the circle using a gold-threaded silk shawl as a shimmering dance partner. Always three or four belly dancers working the crowd while pretending to ignore the crowd.

After sunset, the drummers and dancers set aside the tourist vibe. They light torches and the circle becomes smoky and intense. New people arrive. They drift around the outer fringes of the circle. They pass joints and sometimes pills. They use the drumbeat as a soundtrack to explore each other's bodies…the willing and the woozy. This was usually when Amelia and Phil's group left.

Except one night. It was two winters ago, their final Florida trip together. A little drunk after a few margaritas, Amelia left her group and pushed through the crowd. She entered the circle and started to dance next to a pair of little boys and their yoga-panted mom. The mom's purple crop top exposed smoothly muscled arms, arms that seemed to welcome Amelia as they drew invisible, abstract paintings in the air.

A girl in her twenties joined them. She had a fluorescent hula hoop around her waist that lit up the growing darkness. The hoop moved with her body, over her denim cut-offs and lacy bikini top, even around her neck. Neon green and pink flashed on a bare belly, circled her tanned legs. Then came an older woman, maybe fifty, with gently rounded flesh. Silver coins on her belly dance hip scarf jingled with each graceful turn of her pelvis. Her red lipstick and white teeth glowed in the light of the drummers' torches.

The shawl lady arrived, dipping and diving. Her flying silk enclosed their inner group like a force field. A circle within a circle. The beat intensified and everyone moved faster as they sensed and responded to the movements of nearby bodies. Amelia was in the middle of all of this. She felt herself almost dissolving, like this could go on forever; like they were outside time.

Then the crowd parted and Phil appeared. He wasn't quite dancing but his baby steps had perfect rhythm. He ducked around the shawl lady and took Amelia's hands. For a moment—a split second—Amelia believed they were dancing together, that he was dancing with her. But then she bumped into a tambourine player and realized she was being led out of the circle, away from the group, across the width of beach, through the parking lot, and finally to the lights and a cross-walk on Ocean Boulevard.

"Time to go," Phil said.

Her husband held her hand tightly. Though he never, ever said he was embarrassed, she felt his dismay. And she saw herself: the floral blouse and khaki walking shorts over cotton underpants, her bunioned feet stuffed into New Balance sneakers. White ankle socks.

Phil's wife, age seventy-three, moving her hips and hands in that way in a circle of strangers.

HE LIKES HIS mashed potatoes plain: no salt, no butter. His appetite is rebounding so she constructs the same bland shepherd's pie she has made since their early years, the only flavouring a shake of oregano she sneaks in. This after-noon the chore of peeling potatoes becomes a meditation, allows her to hit the pause button. Amelia feels the grip of the hard steel peeler in her hand, runs her middle finger along its sharp edge, notices a tiny spot of corrosion. She takes her time with each potato, noting how easily the skin comes away if you discover the correct angle, exposing the pale yellow flesh beneath. As the mound of peels grows, she lifts them lightly with both hands and carries them to the compost bin.

Her favourite part is the top layer. She piles potatoes on the ground beef and then levels it like a pastry chef icing a cake. She will replenish Phil's freezer with eight individual meals securely packed in blue-lidded Tupperware when the food cools.

When she is done, Amelia tidies her workspace and arranges her tools in the dishwasher. She walks across the hall to the den to find Phil tilted back in the recliner. He is snoring.

This used to be her chair. Phil surprised her with it after her knee replacement. Researched the technical specifications thoroughly, delivered meals on a tray, brought her books from the library, and ice packs for the swelling.

After she recovered, the chair slowly devolved into Phil's possession. It was more his taste anyway; she preferred the leather couch.

"I should have let you pick," he said to her one day, months after she had moved out. "Or we should have done it together."

HIS PAIN MEDICATION has kicked in and now he is fully out of it. The chair is reclined to its limit, and gentle snorts punctuate his breathing. The fleece blanket has fallen to the floor, and she sees how his shorts are bunched up, exposing clumps of grey bristle on his left ball.

Old man junk. She remembers when the hairs were dark brown, unlike this steel wool. Phil's uncircumcised tip rests on the wrinkles of his sack. The air conditioning has made his dick shrink into itself.

Amelia walks over and slides Phil's penis back into his shorts. The vibrancy of her new nail polish, a deep crimson called *I'm Not Really a Waitress*, contrasts with his pale flesh. He doesn't stir, doesn't react to her touch.

She picks up the blanket from the carpet, covers his lower body, tucks the edges of the throw loosely into the chair creases next to his hips. Then she steps back to assess the situation. This is better, she decides, or at least it will do.

Patches

ANNIE SITS WITH HER PHONE IN HER HANDS AT A SMALL TABLE on the edge of a winery deck on the north shore of Nova Scotia. She is waiting for a man who has no intention of keeping his promise. He'd seemed to be what she was looking for: decent job, grown kids, a genuine smile. Stable.

The Tidal Bay wine bottle is almost empty, but this guy has not messaged, not even to lie. A family emergency or car trouble or an abscessed tooth—any story would have been a kindness. Maybe she'd joined the wrong dating site. They call it a club, but come on. Perhaps other sites attract better humans, but the men she has met in exchange for $43.99 a month are like yard sale jigsaw puzzles. Always a few critical pieces missing, but no way for you to know that until you try to make the whole picture and end up with gaping holes.

The best ones were okay, boring guys she had zero chemistry with, and the worst assumed your mouth would be on them in minutes. Or they bombarded her with unsolicited shots of their middle-aged schlongs. This seemed to be a new kind of pandemic, she and her girlfriends agreed.

And then there were the disappointments. After a promising coffee date with great conversation about movies and books, and then a second hiking date, a well-mannered accountant offered to cook her dinner at his downtown Halifax condo. Before she even swallowed a cracker of supermarket hummus, he was requesting the temporary use of her freshly-manicured feet on his penis.

Asked politely, then implored, and finally begged.

This is what it's like.

Annie turns her phone face down on the table and raises the glass to her lips again. Wonders if she should bother to freshen up and reapply lipstick. She does not have the energy to move. Instead, she watches six groups of Harleys snake down the curving country road to the winery's parking lot. They disrupt the quiet of the vineyard, with its clusters of grapes organized in tidy rows. Each group of bikers has about a half-dozen riders. They follow in staggered formation behind a leader, filling the unpaved parking lot from back to front in tight, evenly spaced intervals.

The winery restaurant pairs their reds, whites, and rosés with artisanal brick-oven pizza and plates of local smoked pork that the menu calls charcuterie. The tourists and cottage country regulars who sit under matching umbrellas on the winery's deck look up from their food and drink; they smile or raise their eyebrows. The people at the table next to Annie attempt witty comments about the motorcycles' arrival.

Some of the bikers ride solo while others carry a passenger. As they remove their helmets, they reveal grey hair, dyed hair, or no hair.

It strikes Annie as too much leather and denim on a sunny, late-summer day.

She had ordered the Tidal Bay and a charcuterie tray at noon. Over the next two hours, the bottle transitioned from full to half-full, reluctantly to half-empty, and then undeniably empty. Piece by piece, the meat and cheese, baguette, olives, and gherkins disappeared from the wooden serving board. Even with all this food in her stomach, Annie knows she should not drive back to the cottage.

The waiter adjusts the overhead umbrella to cover Annie. The sun is hot. She wears no hat and her freckled, bare arms have pinkened.

An hour ago, the waiter told her that he's a musician. Patio season is short, Annie knows, so he's probably anxious to turn this table. And here he is, she thinks, tending to a middle-aged woman who has clearly been stood up and cannot ethically or maybe even legally be served another drink. But she has mentioned that she is a cottager, so he'll understand that she'll be back.

She has just ordered another single glass of wine.

"Someone will pick me up," she says, more to save face and stall than out of any certainty. Reality: She is forty kilometres from her parents' cottage, which she has claimed this weekend while her mother watches the kids. Maybe a neighbour can retrieve her, maybe not.

"Can I bring you an iced tea on the house? Made from scratch," says the waiter.

Annie looks at him and then across to the parking lot, where the riders have finished parking their gleaming motorcycles in neat rows. She feels light-headed, regrets taking the antihistamine. Regrets the pointless worry about sneezing from autumn leaf spores on a first date. Regrets the money and self-respect poured into the dating app.

"Real maple syrup, no sugar," he says.

Some of the machines in the parking lot look to Annie like giant tricycles. Trikes for aging toddlers with red-veined noses and high blood pressure. Later, she'll learn that the third wheel stabilizes the bike and helps aging knees balance 1,200 pounds of Harley, 225 pounds of man, and an extra 147 pounds of passenger on its padded seat.

"We all need to be careful in this heat," says the waiter.

"Sure. Bring it on," says Annie, squinting so that the motorcycles become one shiny blur against the branches and greenery of the grapes. It can be a great comfort when a stranger saves you from yourself.

ANNIE DOESN'T MEAN to knock over the iced tea and the empty wine bottle but when she stands up to go to the bathroom, a stray elbow sets off a chain reaction. The wine bottle falls first. She tries to catch it, but either the bottle or her hands hit the tall, narrow glass, leaving the tabletop a mess of cold tea, ice, and lemon slices. The glass, sticky with dregs, tumbles to the deck. The effort of these attempts takes out her knees, and as Annie lunges for the chair she steps unwisely and falls. Just a few inches to the ground but down she goes.

Moments later, it seems, she hallucinates Lawrence from the office. This hazy version of her fellow economist wears a black leather vest with colourful patches, and Frye boots with faded jeans. He leans over her, as does a bald man with bushy sideburns. This man has a patch on his leather vest that says Smokey.

She lies in the shade on cool grass, legs bent. Lawrence places a rolled-up leather jacket under her head. The bald man with the sideburns holds her wrist and asks questions. Annie feels a cool, wet cloth on her forehead and the slight pressure of fingers on her wrist. A blood pressure cuff appears from nowhere and squeezes her upper arm forever before it suddenly releases.

"It's all good," says Lawrence from the office. Not imagined, it turns out. "Smokey here is a doctor."

ANNIE'S JOB IS to predict how much alcohol and legal weed people will buy so that the provincial government can project its revenues. Summer, autumn, winter, and spring, her quarterly forecasts are spot on. Her boss says it's uncanny, calls her president of an elite club of exactly one.

At work she is the odd man out in a team of odd men. She and Lawrence have worked together for months but she doesn't know much about him. The men on the revenue forecasting team set themselves apart as experts who shine their intellectual light in a cubicle sea of generic civil servants. Annie interprets this as self-preservation. Nerdy males with limited social skills protecting themselves from failing at basic, daily communication with their colleagues.

Lawrence was a new hire from the private sector. He kept his mouth shut for the first few months, and was rewarded with a work friendship with the two other economists. They opened ranks and accepted him into their plaid button-down shirt and khaki pant club. Annie watches them walk past her cubicle together on their way to get coffee every day at ten and two. Sees them huddle in the office kitchen for a brought-from-home lunch at noon, except for payday Thursdays, when they settle into a reserved booth across the street at the Celtic Nook.

Annie eats alone most days. She has salad at her desk or occasionally treats herself to a shawarma from a shop downstairs. Anyway, working through lunch, drinking thermos coffee at her desk, and taking her laptop home means she can leave on time. At ten and twelve, Noah and Julia don't need a babysitter anymore, but she arranges her life to be home shortly after they get off the bus.

She worries that Noah doesn't seem to have any close buddies, and that Julia tries too hard to be everyone's friend.

THE MONDAY AFTER the winery visit, Annie leaves an envelope on Lawrence's desk with money for the wine and food bill she knows he paid. They've agreed to call this her "unfortunate episode." He has already refused the money but Annie wants a clean slate.

A few weeks later, at eight o'clock on a Sunday morning, she parks her Civic at the far end of the Walmart parking lot, and waits. There's a rolled-up yoga mat in the back seat; her mom and the kids think she's at a Yin class. The yoga membership was an unrequested gift from her mother, who last year announced that she did not and had never felt at ease in her own home. Did not belong there. Now, liberated—kind of, there's no divorce—from a forty-nine-year marriage, she spends a few nights a week with a man who is 180 degrees from Annie's engineer father.

But she still devotes every Sunday morning to her grandkids so that her Annie can "live a little."

That's fine with Annie. Julia came home at seven this morning from a sleepover, silent and sullen, after a night of trading her Julia-ness to be part of the pack. Let Julia's grandmother tend to the wounds of a twelve-year-old who has just discovered how vicious girls can be. And let Grandma explain to Noah why the dad who disappeared out west when he was a toddler is too busy for FaceTime.

It was a relief to leave the house. Annie turns off the engine and sinks into the car's quiet warmth. If Lawrence doesn't show up, this should be enough, she thinks. This peace, she bargains, is surely worth the cost.

Walmart has just opened for the day, with early birds parked near the front doors. The only other vehicles at this end of the lot are twin motorhomes with South Carolina licence plates and RV Club of America bumper stickers. Two silver-haired couples sitting on lawn chairs share the space between the trailers. They face each other across a folding table, four bowls and two thermoses between them, and an awning overhead. They play cards and eat cereal, wear track suits and slippers. One of the women has a cat in her lap.

Annie estimates the cost of the giant trailers, determines they sell for least CA$225,000 apiece. She calculates the age and net worth of the seniors, predicts how they vote, and what news channel they watch. They chose to spend the night here when they could have booked a prime spot on the ocean or in the quiet splendour of a national park. Why, she wonders, did they opt to hunker down side by side on the bare pavement?

Now she sees the motorbike come around the curve of the parking lot, its engine cutting through the Sabbath silence. It is a clunky three-wheeled bike, a distant cousin to the chopper from *Easy Rider*, yet its silver paint and glowing metal sparkle in the morning sun.

Lawrence is on time. He arrived when he said he would arrive.

Annie unbuckles her seat belt. Lawrence circles the parking lot but keeps on moving. He disappears behind Walmart, the sound of his motorcycle fading. Annie turns on her engine; air conditioning would feel good.

Lawrence reappears and does a wide turn to steer toward the grocery store, but then vanishes again around the corner. Did he even see her, she wonders, dialling up the fan. She could have been stretching in the yoga studio, one woman lying on a mat surrounded by other women on mats, and that might have felt better, but here she is.

Oh, but there he is, approaching from behind. The rumble of the engine grows closer as he pulls up next to her.

Lawrence wears the same outfit he wore at the winery, the leather jacket that she used as a pillow, overlaid now with the same crested leather vest, and the faded jeans that tuck under his stomach. Same boots. He pulls off his helmet and knocks on her window, and she presses the button to lower it.

"You're here," he says.

"Yes," she says. "This is me."

He gives her a guided tour of the bike, running his hands over the metal as he explains. This is a touring Harley, with a proper passenger seat rest, footrest, and handrails. A motorcycle with three wheels and a trunk.

Someone who plans to always ride alone would not choose this model, Annie deduces. She admires the colour, which he tells her is called Gauntlet Grey.

He asks Annie if she is still up for a tryout.

"Why not," she says, though last night, in a failed attempt to head off rumination, she jotted down a list of reasons "why not" and worries now that "why not" sounds like flirting and wonders if this is a situation where flirting is required, to what extent flirting would be unseemly game-playing, and what, in any case, would constitute flirting given their age and clear lack of effort to appear younger. However, observation and analysis of Lawrence's prior behaviour gives her comfort. His abilities to pick up on verbal cues and body language have not proved a particular strength. This, at least, they have in common.

Lawrence opens the hatch and pulls out a black leather jacket and a helmet. When he'd invited her, he assured her that he had all the gear but told her to wear sturdy boots or sneakers.

"I guess we should talk about safety," he says.

Lawrence tells her being a Harley passenger takes practice. To stay in the correct position, he recommends that she focus on the back of his helmet. The bike will lean as they turn, so it will work best if she looks over his shoulder slightly as they round corners. She can use the handrails after she gets a sense of how the bike accelerates, manoeuvres, and stops.

Annie read up on this online. She should hang on to him around his stomach, squeeze her thighs against his if she feels insecure. The closer she is, the safer they both will be, the article said. But Lawrence does not mention the hanging on, or the squeezing. He instructs her not to grab him by his shoulders or arms.

"Please don't do that."

Instead, hold on loosely around his waist. Loosely.

Also, he says, think counterintuitively.

"Go against what your body wants to do. Relax like a sack of potatoes."

She zips the jacket. It is a ladies' size small. It's tight and she battles with the zipper. She worries about sweating and staining the lining under the arms. The helmet is a struggle too, but Lawrence adjusts and tests the chin strap and deems it a good fit. It is heavier than a bike helmet and has a face visor. It makes her feel like an astronaut.

The safety class continues. He explains the science of proper weight distribution and how to maximize balance and control. He points out that the exhaust pipes heat up.

"Watch yourself," he says. "People have been scalded."

He sits on the Harley, both feet on the ground, grips the handlebar, and applies the front brake so that it's safe for Annie to lift her right leg and climb on the bike. She manages and they are finally ready to go.

Not quite. He wants her to practice getting on and off the machine. "Mounting and dismounting," he calls it.

"Push yourself toward the machine," he explains. "Do not grab, do not pull it toward you."

"Got it," she says after the third round.

He asks if she feels comfortable enough to ride. His view, he says, is that the passenger is in charge. The pilot controls the bike and the passenger controls the pilot.

"Don't be afraid to tap me on the shoulder if I can't hear you."

He starts the motor. The bike's movements are jerky and Annie's helmet bumps into Lawrence's helmet. As they turn corners, she remembers something he said about slow turns being more dangerous than faster turns.

She squeezes her inner thighs subtly into his outer thighs but makes sure she isn't too clingy around his waist. He doesn't react, not that she can notice, so she assumes this must be okay, the correct pressure to be safe but not pushy. Is she having fun? She isn't sure. It's awkward but not awful. Being uncomfortable is a price she is willing to pay.

After the third circuit of the parking lot, Annie briefly shifts her focus from the back of Lawrence's helmet to the couples underneath the trailer awning. Do they see her on the back of this motorcycle? Are they watching? She can't be sure, but believes yes, yes they are.

Bye, bye, she thinks.

THEY NEVER LEAVE the parking lot. After seven passes of a circuit that includes Walmart, Mark's Work Wearhouse, Sobeys, the mall, and the bus terminal, they're back where they started.

Lawrence stops the motor and pauses for a moment before saying, "Ready. Dismount." Annie goes first. It all feels strange, but it's her first time and she can learn. The main thing is, she survived the orientation and the practice ride and is ready to join him on the road.

"Where do we go next?" she asks. She might have to call home and tell them she's having coffee with some yoga people.

Lawrence takes off his helmet. The bandana on his head is damp with sweat.

"This is it," he says. "For today anyway."

The motorhome people have rolled back their awning; they're folding up their table and chairs.

Lawrence tells her he needs to leave now or he'll be late. He has promised to meet the other Orphans' Brothers at a deli on the Herring Cove Road. From there, they will travel as one column and cruise down a peninsula that juts out to the sea. They'll all bring picnic lunches and, after sharing food, they will play bocce ball.

Smokey is president of the Orphans' Brothers club, and road captain for today's trip. He'll be at the front, leading the other riders along the coastal highway. Lawrence is the designated sweep rider for the day, communicating by Bluetooth headset to Smokey in front. It is an important job. He'll be the final bike, riding at the back to make sure no one is left behind. If someone runs into trouble, they can count on him. Jeff, the guy who used to do it, had a stroke, so Lawrence moved up.

"I can't let them down, so, no passengers," he says.

"A promotion. You can't screw it up," says Annie, handing back the jacket.

"I mean, a passenger who isn't experienced," he says as he zips and folds. "It wouldn't be a good idea. Not this time."

"Especially when it's my first try. I mean, if you're riding bitch, you have to know what you're doing,"

She isn't sure if this is an attempt at humour, or casual cool, or god-knows-what, but out it comes.

Lawrence is about to put the tidy bundle back in the hatch, but he stops quickly and looks at her.

"What did you say?"

Too late now to take it back.

"My first time on the bitch seat?"

"No," he says. She sees what she interprets as disappointment in his eyes. "We do not say that. Nobody says that."

He stows away the jacket and closes the lid.

"Of course," she says. "Of course. I'm sorry."

"Anne, you are a passenger. To get technical—a pillion. You sit on a pillion pad."

A pillion. That's what I am, thinks Annie, pulling off her astronaut helmet.

"But I prefer passenger. Or guest," he says.

Lawrence dips and tilts his head. He is roughly seven inches taller than she is, so a deliberate move is necessary to achieve eye contact, which is brief, but definite.

"Or maybe we just call it riding double."

"Sure," says Annie.

Before she leaves, wanting to linger, she asks Lawrence about the crests on his vest.

"Not crests. Patches," he says. "Club patches."

The patch on the left side of his vest shows two hands, connected palm to palm, bent at the knuckles and entwined. The logo is embroidered in sea blue on a black background.

"Links in a chain," Lawrence explains. He makes the same gesture with his own hands, showing how hard it is to pull them apart.

He turns around. A large version of the logo covers most of his back, with *Orphans' Bros International* in crisp white print above it, and *Unbreakable Bond* written below in crimson.

On the right side of his vest, a Canadian flag patch, and below it, a patch that says *Seinfeld*, with simple white letters on a black background.

"My road name. They gave me that a few months ago," he says.

"You're Jewish?"

"No, I'm funny. They think I'm funny."

THAT FIRST SUMMER afternoon at the winery, after the initial confusion had passed and Smokey had determined this was not a medical emergency, Annie rested in the shade of the bikers' picnic tent. She liked it in the cool grass, sitting cross-legged in the shade of the open awning. Friendly women—wives and girlfriends of full-fledged club members—offered her cookies, watermelon, Coke, and mineral water.

Annie rehydrated and snacked, and then, after the novelty of her presence subsided, she laid back and closed her eyes. She imagined she was almost invisible, a creature protected by the camouflage of its coat. Pop cans and plastic containers snapped open. Chip bags rustled. She sensed foot-steps as people trod carefully around her. Snatches of conversations drifted over and around her body. Laughter rolled in and out like ocean ripples on a calm day.

Two couples discussed a plan to take their bikes to Freeport, Maine, and then hop a train to Manhattan to see some plays. Someone inquired if someone else's mother had found a spot in a nursing home.

She overheard Lawrence tell someone she was a friend from work.

And then, a hand on her wrist, warm but light. She opened her eyes to see Smokey checking her pulse again and Lawrence sitting next to her, eating a sandwich. Woozy but now mortified, she began to apologize. An idiot with the anti-histamine, she explained. Stood up by a friend, she said. Not one to usually have more than one glass, she assured them.

"What happens in Vegas," said Lawrence, and then opening his arms to the vineyard, "or on the north shore."

Despite the heat, he was still wearing the leather vest over his white T-shirt. She remembered that the rolled-up jacket under her head was his.

"Who among us," added Smokey. He released the blood pressure cuff and Annie's arm exhaled.

Her vitals were okay.

"You're good to go," he said, "but welcome to stay."

Zone of Significant Impact

SHE DOES NOT WANT IT TO END THIS WAY. SHE DOESN'T WANT IT to end at all. But right now, never mind the oak forest, the vineyards, the olive groves. Emma thinks about the ten thousand wild boar—*cinghiale*—who roam undetected. With every step on the path, these swine watch her. According to *Lonely Planet*, this is their territory, their natural habitat, so they must be near, even if she can't see them.

She and her friends, Andy and Ciara, have left their home base in Lyon for a weekend in Italy. They hike three abreast on a loop that begins and ends in the Tuscan market town of Greve.

These pigs, Emma has read, have heads that occupy a third of their bodies, beady eyes, and bulldozer snouts. They consume anything in their path: plants, roots, leaves, berries, nuts, fruit, worms, lizards, snakes, mice. But the *cinghiale* adore grapes. They'll jump an electric fence and ravage rows of fruit, destroying swathes of vineyard overnight. Grapes that had been nurtured with patience and skill.

The males are silent and solitary, except during breeding season. The females are grunters and more sociable, but never come between a sow and her piglets.

"Just one more tiny question and then I'll shut up about it," Emma says to her friends. "They say if you run into a boar, you should back away calmly. But they also tell you to yell. How does it make sense to do both at the same time?"

Andy and Ciara glance at each other across Emma.

"It means you raise your voice but don't feckin' panic," says Ciara.

Emma knows that being afraid does not mean you are in actual peril. Still, her brain signals that every slight rustling in the bushes is a protective sow or a marauding male. Worry is not reality but is more seductive than logic. She supposes it must be evolutionary, that our fear was once connected to our survival.

She inhales for four seconds, pauses. Exhales for another four to establish a steady rhythm. Hiking is supposed to be relaxing. Hiking is being in nature and nature is good. Nature is real. Why, then, is her nervous system lighting up? Why has it been lighting up for weeks? She grips a thick tree branch with her left hand, uses it as a walking stick. She does not need it for stability, but if a creature attacks, she'll have a defensive option.

Her friends know what she's up to with the "walking stick" but humour her.

"Whatever it takes," Andy said, helping her pick a sturdy limb before they set out on the Tuscan trail.

THEY'RE SETTLED INTO tonight's home, a hostel room with two bunk beds, their usual choice. The trio travels lightly and only packs necessities, but knapsacks and a jumble of clothes litter the spare lower bunk.

Emma lies on an upper bunk prepping an Instagram post. She rations her social media, has purged TikTok and Twitter and pared it down to Insta, the barest minimum, curated with care. The tree branch/weapon, the controlled breathing, the real or imagined creatures lurking in the bushes, none of these will appear in the official record of Emma's Italian weekend. She chooses a close-up of yellow daisies against a blue cloudless sky. Also, a panoramic view of the ancient town of Montefioralle framed by cypress trees. Finally, a glass of Chianti Classico and a pile of grapes resting on a rustic oak barrel. In the background a vineyard, organic. And, of course, a sunset.

Caption: *This was our weekend!*

She expects her father to respond within minutes with hearts and clapping hands, knows her mom will immediately post something like *wish I was there!!!* Her parents separated a few years ago. Dealing with them as individuals is a chore. Especially long-distance; she manages communication with them as carefully as her social media.

As she is about to post, she sees they've each already messaged her. Usually that's a sign of heightened clinginess, but today it is something else. Emma looks down from the hostel bunk at Andy and Ciara. They're sharing a bag of red grapes, spitting the pits into hostel toilet paper, and shopping for cheap Ryanair tickets for their next trip.

"Holy shit, guys, my house is burning down."

Emma climbs down the ladder and gestures for the iPad they share. The screen is a cloudy mess of mingled DNA, smeared with greasy fingers and the residue of their individual body oils, their hand cream, their grapes and olives and walnuts. She squeezes in between Andy and Ciara on the tiled floor and, with a few taps, learns that a nine-hundred-hectare forest fire is burning out of control in a heavily wooded clump of suburbs outside of Halifax, Nova Scotia.

A wildfire.

The home she grew up in, in flames. Maybe. Her whole neighbourhood ablaze. Possibly.

There's a map of the evacuation zone online and her

house is in the centre, but nothing is confirmed. The news reports say there's been no rain in five weeks, the longest stretch in forty Aprils. The trees are parched, the air is bone-dry, and the wind is unrelenting.

The fire is fresh and greedy. It feeds on a buffet of readily available fuel: maple, oak, and evergreen. The houses in Emma's old neighbourhood have large wooden decks overlooking generous backyards. The wind is carrying sparks from roof to roof, and flames leap from treetop to treetop. Conditions are perfect.

The images mesmerize, draw her unwillingly back to a place she has not completely forsaken, but does not miss. Her friends, silent witnesses, don't interrupt as she races between news sites.

The municipality, she reads—out loud now—has declared a state of emergency. Every available firefighter has been called in. Some live in the evacuation zone; they must abandon their own homes to fight for everyone else's. Water bombers are on the way. So far, thirteen thousand people have fled, navigating heavy traffic through smoke and falling ash to escape from suburbs that had been designed with one exit and no fire hydrants.

"Better call home," says Ciara. "Talk to your parents."

"They say they're fine."

"Still," says Ciara. "It *is* your house."

Andy throws a grape at Ciara. "I mean it *was* your house, Em. Sorry."

"Is my house, was my house." She's still pissed that they put it on the market a few weeks after she left town.

"Both true," she says.

They sit together on the floor of their Italian hostel, hypnotized by images captured by strangers 5,600 kilometres away. They watch flames spread along the gently curved avenues of a woody Canadian suburb, a neighbourhood where nature is welcomed—when it knows its place. The uncontrolled inferno may or may not have already destroyed the homes on the street where Emma learned to ride a bike, leaving melted, cracked pavement.

"That is some surreal shit," says Ciara, tapping the screen so that it fills.

They find a series of TikToks posted by a roofer. His crew is finishing a job, hammering down the final few shingles on a two-storey home, cleaning up the worksite, all of them sweating in the unseasonal early May heat. Then the trees in the yard next door ignite.

The anonymous roofer pulls out his phone and starts to shoot: "Shit. There's a bush fire."

The situation escalates quickly and soon he uploads a new video. Flames shooting up from thirty-foot evergreen trees.

"Somebody's pool is about to light up!" he says as the fire encroaches on a stack of lounge chairs surrounding an empty above-ground swimming pool. In the next video, he begs a man in a white dress shirt and tie to run. The man is clumsily unfurling a garden hose to defend his home against the approaching wall of fire.

"Time to go, buddy," he yells, as he runs toward the stranger, still filming.

"It's not worth it, man," he implores.

In his final post, the roofer shoots out of his truck window as his crew escapes. He focuses on the tidy beige house they're leaving behind, where they've laboured for long days.

"Friggin' roof's finally done."

In the distance, sirens scream.

ANDY, WHO GREW up in an apartment in Mexico City, cannot believe the masses of trees surrounding these homes.

"Did you live in a forest?"

"Kind of," says Emma. They had a two-acre lot just like everyone else and a backyard where Emma had helped her mother grow tomatoes, zucchini, and carrots.

"I had a tree house," she says. Emma pulls up a photo on her phone.

"Look."

It must have been autumn; the leaves were lit up in reds and golds and oranges. A ten-year-old Emma looks down from an eight-foot-high platform, protected by a railing.

Andy reaches for the phone. "Looks like a real house," she says. "People could live there. A whole family."

"Dad built it from scratch. Anchored it with concrete posts."

"Did you go up there in the winter?" Andy adores Canadian weather horror stories.

"If it was icy, no. But rainy days, yes. The roof never leaked. Mom said it was better built than our house."

She takes the phone back from Andy.

"Hope it's still there," Emma says. "For whoever."

"You really should ring them," says Ciara.

"My father thinks he would've been happier as a carpenter instead of an accountant," says Emma.

She shuts off her phone.

"I'll call tomorrow."

"It's just dinner time there, isn't it, Em?"

"I'm wiped. Not tonight."

AFTER THEY TURN off the lights, she lies on her upper bunk under a thin sheet and imagines fighting the wildfire. A thick hose connected to a bottomless lake, and her standing in front of the blaze. The big house and the little house are behind her, safe. She defends her childhood bedroom, decorated in multiple variations of purple. Mauve, violet, magenta, lilac, orchid, amethyst, all echoing her favourite clothes. It is/was a wild mix of patterns, florals, and stripes.

The fire is relentless. It escalates into an inferno. The hose she uses to fend it off grows heavy. Eventually, Emma drifts into dreamless sleep.

THE NEXT DAY they're back in Lyon, home again after an early-morning bus, another bus, a thirty-six-euro flight and two more buses.

The regional high school where they work offers specialized programs and has a residence for out-of-town students and the language teaching assistants. Emma, Ciara, and Andy's suite has a bedroom for each of them, and they share a kitchenette and a tiny living room with generic dorm furniture. They've added bits and pieces from the flea market: a green glass table lamp, an orange wool throw for the couch, a few framed, antique family portraits mysteriously relinquished by their original owners. They'll leave these treasures behind when they scatter at the end of May, going their separate ways after almost two years together.

On the couch, Emma cuddles under the orange throw and calls her father on WhatsApp. Andy and Ciara are at the gym.

It's late morning in Eastern Canada. Her father is at work so he closes his office door. Holding the camera too close to his face, he says it is another rainless, windy, stinking hot day and the fire has mushroomed. More neighbourhoods have been evacuated. Because the fire started on a Sunday afternoon, he says, many people were out and blocked from coming back.

He picks at a greying eyebrow with his thumb and index finger.

"No chance to go home again," he says.

"Is our place okay?"

He pauses. "I just don't know."

His hair is longer than it used to be, and he seems to be attempting some type of beard, its fresh bristles unattractive close up. He strokes the burgeoning, undefined facial hair.

"I showed Ciara and Andy the tree house."

"I'm sorry, sweetie."

She nods and asks him about the map she saw online that shows the perimeter of the fire evacuation site in yellow, and within it, a "Zone of Significant Impact" in orange. Their street is orange.

"I saw that too. Maybe it changed, though. Fires can shift."

SHE HASN'T BEEN back to Canada in sixteen months, not even this past Christmas. Instead, she bunked down with Andy at Ciara's parents' house in Dublin.

"Let's try someone else's family," she said to Andy when they were invited.

"Can't be worse than home," Andy replied.

Emma and Andy slept across from Ciara, taking turns on the second twin bed and the floor. Adding up Ciara's sisters and brothers, two grandmothers, and assorted other relatives and friends, there were nineteen at dinner. Ciara's parents set up folding tables in the living room and they drank prosecco from plastic cups with their lukewarm turkey and roast vegetables. Their heaping plates overflowed with rich brown gravy.

Emma last saw her father in person in August, when he visited her in Lyon. He stayed in a rental, arriving with a Tripadvisor must-see checklist that included an indoor market named after a famous chef. Her father is a self-described foodie so a pilgrimage to the market was nonnegotiable. He was surprised to learn Emma had never been there.

"I'll take you to a grocery store if you want 'authenticity,'" she said.

"We can do that too, to compare."

"Compare what?"

As they pushed through the aisles of the indoor food hall, jammed with people who Emma suspected were mostly tourists, unappealing images assaulted her. Oysters that looked like squashed eyeballs resting on a grimy shell. Rooster heads, red coxcomb and feathers intact, still attached to pale-skinned corpses. Pig ears and feet, hooves really. Pâté with chunks of congealed fat. Piles of fish livers, beige and slimy. Runny cheeses that appeared to be covered in gravel.

Her father stopped at a display of tiny, grey-furred rabbits curled together as if they were cuddled up and napping.

"Look. Real food," said her father. "At home, we forget where it comes from."

"We don't eat much meat," said Emma, as she crossed over to reach the fruit and vegetables.

"These cherries cost three times what we pay at Monoprix."

She inspected a four-euro artichoke.

"And we buy veggies at the neighbourhood market for cheap."

"Let me treat you and the girls. Pick whatever you want."

Emma looked at her father across the aisle. The artichoke was a globe in her hand, moist, its tightly packed leaves topped with miniature thorns. Her dad was still staring at the dead rabbits. She thought of how she and her friends would dip the artichoke's tender, steamed leaves in a tangy sauce, of how they would chop the heart for salads. She waited until her dad looked at her again and then smiled her smallest smile, attempting to radiate both judgment and non-judgment at the same time.

"What? Oh, sorry. You and your friends."

After shopping, they went their separate ways, Emma with paper bags containing food he'd bought for her to share: a half-kilo of almonds, three varieties of apple, the pricey cherries, a bag of red, yellow, and purple tomatoes, two organic artichokes, and several chunks of single origin dark chocolate. Her father had returned to his rental with a meat and cheese platter, a baguette, a bottle of Pinot Noir, and a sack of strawberries. Because Emma had to rush back to work, they'd agreed to meet for supper at a Michelin-starred bistro on his list. They never made it to Emma's neighbourhood grocery store.

AFTER SHE FINISHES her WhatsApp call with her father, Emma teaches her afternoon English Conversation class. This is her favourite; they're about to graduate and are only a few years younger than she is. She'd planned to get them talking about climate change but that discussion leads to the Canadian fires. Emma finds some CBC news coverage and projects it on the classroom's big screen.

The piece features shaky video from a middle-aged couple as they describe their escape from their burning street. As they flee, the husband lifts his camera to the sky.

"That's the sun," he says, in wonder. A yellow incandescent bulb surrounded by a strawberry halo, blending to orange. It looks like high-quality CGI. Then the blue sky surrounding this radiance darkens and swallows its glow. It seems that day turns suddenly to night.

The couple presses on, the wife at the wheel.

"Don't be afraid. Don't worry," the man says.

On both sides of the road, the earth is transformed to red-hot barbecue coals. Sparks blow across the windshield.

"Want me to drive?"

"I can drive," the woman answers as the orange taillights of another vehicle materialize in the darkness. They're too close. The car lurches as she stomps on the brakes.

"You're okay. It's okay," her husband says.

The smoke creates a total eclipse as they navigate a corridor of fire. Flames spew from the tops of the trees on either side of them. The fire has jumped the road.

"Haul ass," he says. "Go, go, go."

"We're okay," she says.

The couple stops speaking as red embers blanket the windshield. The car ahead accelerates and they keep up the pace.

"Wow," says one of Emma's students.

"Allez, allez," says another to the screen.

The class watches the black smoke gradually thin. It morphs to grey and finally to wisps of white. The car emerges into a four-way intersection, into daylight, and a police officer waves them to safety.

"We're out."

"Good work, good work, honey."

Emma minimizes the video.

"'Haul ass,'" says Emma. "It means get out of here, fast, right now. But do not say that, okay? It is not a normal phrase. Not polite."

"D'accord, Mademoiselle."

AFTER CLASS, EMMA walks across the street to a small park, sits on a bench under a tree, and calls her mother. A miniature version appears on Emma's screen. She is working from home today.

"Are you watching the fire?" her mom asks.

Emma feels as if she is in two places at once. She runs her hands along the bench's wooden slats. *I chose this bench*, she thinks. She looks up at oak leaves. Sees the sun that filters through, feels its warmth on her bare arms. She scuffs her feet on the pea gravel under her sneakers.

Be here, now, she reminds herself.

"I'm watching, as best I can," Emma says. "Is the smoke really bad?"

"Really bad. We're supposed to stay inside."

Her small-screen mother's gaze shifts. Her mom, like her dad, just can't figure out where the camera lens is. "Let's talk about you," she says to a nonexistent someone sitting next to Emma.

"What category, Mom? What aspect of me are you interested in?"

"School ends soon, right? When are you coming home?"

"I'm not sure I think of it as home anymore."

She has been trying to be more direct with her mother.

"Not your home? What's that supposed to mean?"

But the truth does not always work in parental interactions. Emma knows this. Sometimes you need to say what they want to hear.

"Just that this has been such a great life experience, you know, like you said it would be. When you suggested I apply."

"But it was never supposed to be permanent. Your French work visa runs out soon, right?"

"I like who I am here," says Emma. "When I'm not there."

Her mother nods. "What are your options?"

"Tutoring. Working under the table. Maybe here, maybe somewhere else. We'll see."

Emma wishes she was as blasé as she's trying to sound. What if this time in France turns out to be the best part of her whole life?

"What are Ciara and Andy doing next?"

"Andy, law school in Spain. Ciara is going home, back to uni to finish."

"Is there something else keeping you there? Or someone? A guy?"

Emma wonders if her mom told her own mother the intimate details that she now expects Emma to spill.

"Seriously?"

EMMA WILL NEVER confide about Emma the Amnesiac.

Barcelona. Waking up in a curtained cubicle in a hospital bed, an IV in her arm, head pounding, nauseous. Andy and Ciara sitting on folding chairs. No clear memory—then or now—of how she ended up here. That was some other girl, who, according to her friends, accepted a drink from a stranger, slurred her words, collapsed on the dance floor.

Every now and then Emma reconstructs their hospital conversation, still a blur. Remembers, maybe imagines, drifts through, and then lets it go.

"We think some Texan arsehole poisoned you," Ciara might have said that morning.

"My fault," Andy might have added. "He was lurking. I didn't like his vibe so I said, 'Sorry dude. She's in a situationship.'"

Andy would have been referring to François, the engineering student in Lyon. At first he and Emma hooked up a few times a week, now only when they were drunk or bored.

When Emma connected with someone else, someone interesting, like the Australian singer-songwriter with the ridiculous hair in Amsterdam, it wasn't cheating. The thing with François was super casual.

But the Texan, Andy said, had been offended to receive a preemptive rejection via a Mexican with multiple piercings. "He said, 'I'll buy her a drink and we'll see.'"

"Those bouncers threw us out instead of helping," Andy continued, in Emma's reconstructed version. "For a tiny skinny person, you were super heavy."

They'd rushed to the hospital, Ciara explained. It wasn't busy but they'd waited for hours, until Emma puked on the waiting room bench.

The ER doctor checked her pupils, her blood pressure, ordered blood tests, assured her she was safe. He kept her in the hospital until the afternoon to make sure she was stable. He looked like the older, tired version of someone famous, she wasn't sure who, and he'd asked—she remembered this part clearly, she was coming back to herself at that point—did she live in Barcelona?

"No. We're from Lyon."

The doctor crinkled his brown eyes. "French citizens? Really?"

"We work there. For now."

Had she reddened or had she been too sick to blush?

"Right. You can be from wherever you want, but the front desk will insist on immediate payment, and a permanent address for the receipt."

In the end, he filled out the forms so there was no overnight charge, but the bill was still 180 euros for emergency, non-resident, care.

"This is the minimum," he said. "Good luck with the billing department."

Emma didn't want paperwork of any kind sent back to Canada. "We have coverage in France from work," she tried to explain to a guy their age behind glass at the billing office. There were monthly deductions from her paycheque but the sécurité sociale still hadn't sent a health card.

Andy tried, this time in Spanish, but an exchange that seemed too long for the subject ended in mutual shrugs.

"He says we pay. He'll give us a receipt today and maybe, probably not, France will reimburse you. He says French insurance only works in Spain if you're French. Not us."

It was a few days before payday and Emma's Mastercard was at the limit, so Andy and Ciara split the bill between their own credit cards.

"I'll need this back," said Ciara.

"Of course."

EMMA KNOWS SHE'LL never share that story with her mother, whether they're in the same room, same house, same town, or, as now, an ocean and a chunk of continent apart.

She stares at her mom on the tiny screen. Grey roots along her side part. Her face is puffy. She looks like someone pretending to be not sad. Emma wishes Mom knew that coming home won't fix whatever each of them is going through.

"No," she says. "There's no guy 'keeping me' here."

"I shouldn't even be asking."

"No, you shouldn't. And it's weird that you haven't mentioned the house. Our house."

Her mother shakes her head.

"It's because it's gone, Emma. Fire or no fire, it's gone. We had no choice."

"Oh, you two had plenty of choice."

Six weeks after she'd left Canada, her parents put the

house on the market. They sold it eight days later. Her mother packed up Emma's room and stacked the boxes in her new condo's spare bedroom closet. That first Christmas, Emma flew home and spent an uncomfortable ten days shuttling between her parents' separate households.

"Sorry we're not perfect."

Don't take the bait, Emma cautions herself. *Don't bite. Resist further degeneration into your snippy teen years.*

"The fire," she says. "They're saying that barbecues are exploding on decks and then the houses go up."

Emma waits. Her mother looks at her as if she is expecting more.

"The tree house."

"He did a good job on that," her mother concedes.

"Let me know right away, ok? Let me know as soon as you have information?"

"I'll try. Yes."

"Please don't spew meaningless crap to placate me, Mom."

"Look, Emma, I'm not going to drive through police barricades. But when it's safe we'll find out."

"Fair enough," says Emma. She feels the surge deflating as she blows her mother a kiss. She watches Mom do the same from the other side. Then disconnecting, leaving Emma alone on her park bench in Lyon, sheltered by a canopy of oak leaves.

FROM WHAT EMMA could see, her parents' grievances with each other had been petty and childish. No cheating, no real crises. They hadn't even tried marriage counselling. Just gave up. Her eighteen-year-old students, even the boys, were more mature.

There had been no gambling, no wild drinking, no abuse. No coercive control. No gaslighting. They weren't even rude to each other. Instead, it seemed like they both woke up on the same morning, decided they were unhappy, and that the only possible reason for that misery must be this other person sleeping right over there.

"Your father never took me to the movies," her mother said the day her dad moved out.

"Are you kidding?" Emma said.

Her father called Emma that same night and rambled on about self-fulfillment.

"There's no spark. We need to be apart to grow," he'd said.

She wondered, was that elder Gen X code for "boring sex life"? Still, after almost twenty-five years, was that really a deal breaker? What did these people expect?

She pictures them still together, still there, in the house. When the wildfire threatened and the evacuation order came, they would have fled the burning forest as a team, with mere minutes to pack a car. She sees her mother running to rescue Waddle, her stuffed penguin, a black-and-white-and-orange outlier in Emma's purple bedroom. Shoving it into a knapsack along with that ugly chipped vase from the mantle, the one with pastel tissue paper flowers from a long-ago Mother's Day, and her wedding pearls. Sees her father emptying the den bookcase of old photo albums, tearing her high school grad picture from the wall. Frantically, she hopes, rummaging through the winter closet for the scratchy yellow scarf his wife knitted for him. They would have been forced to decide on the spot what was truly important and what was excess, and then to abandon a houseful of accumulated replaceables.

They would have driven away together in one vehicle, leaving the second car to burn in the paved double driveway.

Instead, they're each watching the fire alone in their new homes. She has settled into a generic condo on the edge of the city, while he is renting an overpriced, run-down Victorian flat near the universities. They each claim to be satisfied with their individual choices.

"The building is concrete construction, not wood-framed, very safe."

"I can walk everywhere, so many new restaurants downtown. I'll take you to my favourite wine bar next time you're here."

Their only stated regret is that they sold the family home just months before the real estate market ignited. Imagine, an extra $100,000 that didn't exist, then did, then didn't. Vaporized in front of their eyes.

"Everything is timing." Both of them mouthed the exact same line to her in different conversations. Here, they agreed.

EMMA'S ENGLISH CONVERSATION class is watching the Canadian fire again on the big screen. With the school year winding down, she's running out of ideas to spark discussion and all week she has been preoccupied, getting sucked into way too much wildfire social media.

Her parents still have no news of the old house, or if they do, they're not sharing yet. According to news reports it finally rained last night. It wasn't the torrential downpour they needed, just a few hours of raindrops, but enough to stall the fire's growth. It's still an active blaze but at least the fire-fighters and water bombers can make inroads. There's hope that perhaps the fire can be contained soon, but at the same time, confirmed reports of damage are emerging. Hundreds of homes have been reduced to ash and rubble.

The deputy fire chief appears on the classroom screen. He points to a map showing where the lost homes are.

Emma's street is still in the middle of the orange circle of destruction. He says that even here all is not lost, because the devastation is haphazard. Assessment crews report charred skeletons of minivans in the driveways of intact homes. Garages with patches of melted siding sit next to the remnants of house foundations. Flattened split-entries and, thirty feet away, wooden play structures with swings hanging limply from metal chains.

Miraculously, the deputy chief says, a few homes in the centre of the wildfire have been spared. Flames skipped over a roof or two and leaped into a neighbour's yard.

"The destruction is random," he says, nodding to the reporters. "Directed by the wind. Where it carried the embers, where they landed, what sort of fuel was there."

The deputy chief has been at this for five days. He looks exhausted but keeps flat and calm with his updates. Just the facts and the press release for today. He describes only the reality the crews find on the ground.

Emma taps "pause," reverses to the map, and freezes the shot. She stands in front of the students and touches the classroom screen itself, her finger on the orange zone that the deputy chief is also pointing to. The shadow of her hand covers the deputy chief's hand under the projector's digital glow.

"I used to live right there, right here, when I was a little girl," she tells the class.

"You have not mentioned," says Andrée, one of her front row students who always has something to say.

"But it not my home anymore. I picture it, maybe on fire. I worry about who is there now. I hope they are safe."

When she talks to them, she tries always to be slow and clear. Always complete sentences.

Hakeem raises his hand from the back of the room. He arrived midyear, and is new to Lyon, probably new to France. He is usually quiet, watches and listens to his classmates, only speaks when Emma prompts him.

"No one has been killed, Mademoiselle?" he says. "The news says no one has died."

"That's right."

"They still have their land?"

"Yes, they still have their land. Thank you, Hakeem."

Emma's fingers float back to her keyboard. "One more clip, I think," she says and picks one she watched just before class.

"Do we even have a home to return to?" asks a man wearing a Toronto Maple Leafs ball cap and a Roots t-shirt. He and his wife stand in front of a silver Gulfstream travel trailer that stretches out of the camera frame.

"That's the question."

His wife pushes up her glasses, runs her hand through short grey hair.

"We've seen fires like this in other places. And earthquakes and landslides and whatnot. I always thought, 'Those poor people.' Never dreamt it could happen here."

"Now, we are those people," the man says, putting his arm around her.

"Enough," says Emma, clicking off the video, even though her students' faces have lit with interest, and Hakeem's hand has shot up again. She now sees all the ways this clip could be a gift in English Conversation class. It could ignite discussions about privilege, global inequality, and, especially, how their/her generation is being ripped off.

But she doesn't have the energy for that today. Just isn't up for it.

"Let's talk about how we will all spend the summer," she says.

Despite a low collective groan and a sea of eye rolls, she plows on.

"I will go first. My friends and I will pack up our apartment this weekend. Does anyone want an ugly green lamp?"

The students laugh. She'll miss this captive audience, the way she has always felt at ease here, ever since her first day on the job.

"Then we are going to visit Greece for a few weeks. We will take ferries to our favourite islands. We will eat octopus. We will swim."

She doesn't add that, in Greece, they'll sleep late and lie in a tight row on hot sand under a blazing sky until sunset. Then they'll shower at the hostel and find somewhere to dance until the sun rises again. Scan the beach and hostel and club for attractive people to sleep with, if they feel like it.

Maybe, Emma hopes, they can brainstorm potential futures as they empty jug after jug of retsina that smells vaguely like Pine-Sol. The wine is so cheap, and at first, it burns. But it works and there's always enough to last until the night is over.

"Et puis?"

"English please, Andrée."

"And then? Will you return to Canada?"

"Good question," she says. "I will visit for sure. And maybe stay."

She thinks about the boxes, her belongings, that her mother stores in the new condo's spare bedroom. Wonders how she'll feel tearing off the tape and seeing what they decided to keep of her life. Wonders what will be missing. And if any of it matters.

"Or maybe not go back," says Emma. "Maybe continue school somewhere, somewhere else far away from there, from here, oui?"

"Oui, Mademoiselle. Et puis? Sorry. And *then?*"

"Then, I could become a real teacher. Maybe."

"Oui, Mademoiselle."

Emma looks at the rows of faces.

"I am not worried," she tells them. They all seem so young, except for Hakeem. Only a few years behind her, but she can see the gap between who they are right now and who they will be for the rest of their lives.

"So many things are going to happen," she says. "But I am not worried. I am not worried about any of it."

Acknowledgements

EARLIER VERSIONS OF SEVERAL STORIES APPEARED IN CANADIAN literary journals: "Rescuing Spiderman" originally appeared in the *Humber Literary Review*. "Lost Purse" appeared in *carte blanche*, and "Extermination" was in *The Nashwaak Review*. *The New Quarterly* (TNQ) published "Is This My Christine?" A version of "Patches," titled "Club Patch," was featured on yolkliterary.ca.

Alexander MacLeod edited this collection. He has shared his deep knowledge of the art of short fiction with a generous spirit, and I can't thank him enough.

Thank you to Alissa York and the Humber School for Writers, and to my Humber mentor, Danila Botha, whose vivid sense of story sharpened my work.

As a participant in the Alistair MacLeod Mentorship Program, I appreciate the support of the Writers' Federation of Nova Scotia (WFNS) under the stellar leadership of Marilyn Smulders.

Susan LeBlanc is a wonderful friend and exceptional writer with a keen critical eye and a gift for asking the right questions. Beverly Shaw and Katie Cameron are talented writers whose close reading and thoughtful observations also made these stories better. Thanks also to the Seaport Writers group, as well as Christine Soucie Madill and Wendy Mugridge.

Thank you to Whitney Moran, at Vagrant Press, for her kindness and competence.

A thank you to my siblings, Annie, Pete, and Ruthie, for cheering me on. Our parents, John and Greta Murtagh, raised us in a book-loving home with lively dinner conversation. Our mom continues to inspire.

For Sandy, my husband and best friend. Your love fortifies. And for our Katie, whose courage, keen intellect, and tender heart astound us every day.

And for Ben, always.